"Stop now, [

Stazy pulled away, her cheeks flushed, her breathing erratic. "I'm sure one of your brothers—or possibly both of them!—has told you never to mix business with pleasure!"

He didn't move, only the slight tensing of his jaw showing he wasn't as unmoved by the kisses they had just shared as he would like to appear. "Probably," he acknowledged dismissively. "Prince or frog, Stazy?"

"Is that the reason you kissed me? To see if you could change my mind about that?"

Jarrett, Jonathan and Jordan
are

Some men are *meant* to marry!

Meet three brothers: Jarrett is the eldest, Hunter by name, hunter by nature. Jonathan's in the middle and a real charmer; there's never been a woman he wanted and couldn't have.
Jordan is the youngest and he's devilishly attractive, but he's determined never to succumb to emotional commitment.

These bachelor brothers appear to have it all—looks, wealth, power.... But what about love? That's where Abbie, Gaye and Stazy come in. As Jarrett, Jonathan and Jordan are about to discover—wanting a woman is one thing, winning her heart is quite another!

CAROLE MORTIMER

To Be a Bridegroom

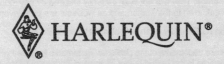

HARLEQUIN®

TORONTO • NEW YORK • LONDON
AMSTERDAM • PARIS • SYDNEY • HAMBURG
STOCKHOLM • ATHENS • TOKYO • MILAN • MADRID
PRAGUE • WARSAW • BUDAPEST • AUCKLAND

If you purchased this book without a cover you should be aware that this book is stolen property. It was reported as "unsold and destroyed" to the publisher, and neither the author nor the publisher has received any payment for this "stripped book."

ISBN 0-373-12051-6

TO BE A BRIDEGROOM

First North American Publication 1999.

Copyright © 1999 by Carole Mortimer.

All rights reserved. Except for use in any review, the reproduction or utilization of this work in whole or in part in any form by any electronic, mechanical or other means, now known or hereafter invented, including xerography, photocopying and recording, or in any information storage or retrieval system, is forbidden without the written permission of the publisher, Harlequin Enterprises Limited, 225 Duncan Mill Road, Don Mills, Ontario, Canada M3B 3K9.

All characters in this book have no existence outside the imagination of the author and have no relation whatsoever to anyone bearing the same name or names. They are not even distantly inspired by any individual known or unknown to the author, and all incidents are pure invention.

This edition published by arrangement with Harlequin Books S.A.

® and TM are trademarks of the publisher. Trademarks indicated with ® are registered in the United States Patent and Trademark Office, the Canadian Trade Marks Office and in other countries.

Visit us at www.romance.net

Printed in U.S.A.

CHAPTER ONE

WHAT on earth was she *doing* here?

Stazy looked around the room, shaking her head in self-disgust. She realised she didn't know a single person here, save for the man at her side—and then she barely knew him, even though he was responsible for bringing her along!

They had spoken for the first time only yesterday—previous polite good mornings or good evenings, if they had happened to meet in the lift or corridor, did not count as speaking in Stazy's book!—and yet here she was, at a family wedding with him.

Boredom had a lot to answer for, she decided, and loneliness. And, for some reason, yesterday she had been feeling both rather acutely.

She had been aware that the man who occupied the neighbouring apartment to her own was called Jordan Hunter, had seen his name over a security button downstairs. But apart from that she knew absolutely nothing more about him. Or he her. But yesterday, for some unknown reason, she had been feeling vulnerable and in need of company...

She couldn't have been more surprised when they had arrived here together this evening and she'd discovered she was a guest at the wedding reception of Jordan's brother Jonathan! Getting through the meal had been awful enough, Jordan silent at her side, but at least she'd had someone seated on her other side to talk to, a man who'd identified himself as Jordan's uncle. Except he hadn't stopped talking, totally monopolising her attention through every course, so that she'd hardly had a chance to eat her food, let alone look at the other guests! But now the meal was over, and everyone had moved into an adjoining room, where a band at one end played music the wedding invitees could dance to.

That was the real problem now; Jordan was just as silent and taciturn as he had been at the table. How quickly could she escape? Stazy wondered impatiently.

She wished she had never responded to his attempt at conversation yesterday!

'How do you like your apartment?'

Since only the two of them stood in the lift, Stazy had known Jordan Hunter had been talking to her! And, considering she had occupied the apartment next door to his for the last three months, the question seemed a little late in coming. Neighbours tended to be a little more friendly back home...

'I like it just fine,' she answered dismissively, grateful when the lift doors opened at their floor and they could step out into the corridor.

'You're American.' It was a statement, and a slightly surprised one at that.

Stazy had been about to walk away, having already taken her keys from her bag, a confused look on her face as she looked up at Jordan Hunter. She had expected him to leave too, but he hadn't moved after he'd stepped out of the lift.

He was, she acknowledged, by any woman's standards, extremely good-looking. Tall, several inches taller than her own five feet nine inches, with curly hair that seemed, she recalled, to have a permanently tousled look, almost as if he were constantly running his fingers through its dark length.

Aged probably in his mid-thirties, more than ten years older than her own twenty-one years, he had the assurance and sophistication to match his maturity; in fact, Stazy had never seen him dressed in anything other than one of the numerous tailored suits he seemed to possess, with pristine shirts and matching silk ties. By contrast, he had probably never seen her wearing anything but jeans or leggings, matched with loose tops, her copper-red hair usually flowing loosely down her spine.

Jordan's face was like a ruggedly hewn sculpture, with a square jaw, firm, unsmiling mouth—although the laughter lines visible beside his eyes and lips said he didn't always look this grim!—and a long, slightly arrogant nose. His eyes she had been saving until last—because they were the most unusual colour Stazy had ever seen! Too light in colour to be called brown, they were actually gold, and surrounded by the thickest, darkest lashes imaginable.

Stazy had noticed all this about him a couple of days after she moved in. But only abstractly. Men, she had decided, were a treacherous bunch of rogues. A totally different species. Probably from a different planet, too, totally incompatible with women. And so Jordan Hunter's good looks had been noted—and then dismissed.

'Yes, I'm American,' she confirmed dryly. She knew all about English reserve, but by practically ignoring her existence for the last three months she felt Jordan Hunter had been taking it too far. For all the notice he had taken of her, she could have been lying dead in the apartment next door to his for that length of time, and he would never have known about it!

He seemed to be taking in her appearance for the first time as he slowly looked her up and down. So much for his only ever having seen her in leggings and loose tops—this man hadn't actually registered her at all until this moment!

She was wearing neat brown ankle boots, fitted denims, a light blue sweatshirt, her hair, as usual, flowing riotously down the length of her back. Her eyes were blue, her nose small and snub, with a peppering of freckles across its bridge, her mouth wide and smiling, her chin pointed. Determined even, she hoped!

'Are you busy tomorrow evening?'

Stazy wasn't quite sure what she had expected his next comment to be—if there was one!—but she certainly hadn't anticipated that. Which was probably the reason why she blurted out, 'No,' before she had given herself the time to think!

Which was how she now found herself standing at his side in the middle of this crowded room!

She had hastily tried to retract that bald statement yesterday, but Jordan had chosen to talk over it, telling her of a party he had to attend, and to which he would like to invite her as his guest. She would have fun, he had assured her as she'd looked unimpressed, meet lots of new people.

What he had omitted to tell her was that the 'party' was, in fact, his older brother Jonathan's wedding reception—and so far the only person she had 'met' had been their garrulous uncle, whose name she couldn't even remember!

The wedding itself had taken place late that afternoon, but now it was all turning into a party. Not that Stazy felt in the least underdressed for the evening, wearing a midnight-blue dress that showed off the perfection of her slender figure, and the tanned length of her long legs. No, it wasn't the way she looked that made her feel so uncomfortable; she just knew, as partner of the groom's brother, that she was attracting more than her own fair share of attention.

She would have fun, Jordan had told her. Being stared at like the specimen in a jar was not her idea of fun! And as for meeting lots of new people, apart from his uncle, Jordan's scowls seemed to be keeping everyone away from them. At least, no one had yet attempted to talk to them...

Stazy wondered again why Jordan had invited her at all. She had given up trying to answer why she had accepted! But Jordan was a good-looking man, could have had his pick of partners for this evening—so why her? The glaringly obvious answer to that was that she didn't know anyone here, and so, in consequence, none of these people knew her either. They might feel curious about her for tonight, but when she didn't appear again they would as quickly forget about her...

But why had Jordan needed to bring a partner with him this evening? What possible reason could he have—?

He was looking darkly across the room at the newly married couple as they danced together, just the sight of his new sister-in-law in her wedding dress seeming to make his expression deepen. Was it possible he was in love with her? Gaye was certainly beautiful enough— tall and blonde, delicately lovely. But if Jordan was in love with his brother's new wife, it was obvious from the way Gaye only had eyes for Jonathan that she didn't return those feelings!

Could it be a love triangle?

Jordan certainly gave every impression of wishing himself a hundred miles away from here, of wanting to be anywhere else but at this family wedding!

Stazy couldn't say she exactly liked being used as a smoke-screen, but if she really was here for that purpose Jordan was doing a lousy job of playing her partner! Several people were now giving them more than enquiring looks, and although she had tried to ignore it for the last five minutes a rather attractive couple standing several feet away now seemed as if their curiosity had got the better of them, and they were going to come over and talk to them!

She turned impulsively to Jordan. 'Would you like to dance?' she prompted quickly; several other couples besides the bride and groom were on the dance floor.

Jordan looked at her blankly for several seconds—almost as if he had forgotten who she was! The man was doing wonders for her self-esteem. And to think she was trying to help him!

'Dance, Jordan?' she repeated. 'The music plays fast or slow—' She paused to listen to the band. 'In this case slow,' she continued mockingly. 'And we human beings—strange creatures that we are!—move in time to it. It really is quite easy—'

'I know what dancing is, Stazy,' he snapped irritably.

Oh, he knew what it was—he obviously just had no intention of doing it!

Ah, well, she had tried, she told herself as she saw the attractive couple fast approaching them...

'Enjoying yourself, Jordan?' It was the man who spoke, tall and dark, arrogantly assured, his glance resting curiously on Stazy as he spoke. A golden-eyed gaze!

Another Hunter, Stazy realised, which meant this had to be the oldest brother, Jarrett. Jordan had at least briefly filled her in on family relations before they came. Good of him! The beautiful dark-haired woman at Jarrett's side had to be his wife, Abbie, a former model.

They had two children around somewhere too, Stazy recalled vaguely—a little girl called Charlie, and a baby boy called Conor.

'Not particularly.' Jordan answered his brother curtly, still scowling.

Jarrett smiled, instantly dispelling that air of arrogance. 'No, I forgot—weddings aren't your favourite things, are they?' he drawled before turning to smile warmly at Stazy. 'I hope you'll forgive my little brother for not introducing us—he seems to have left his manners at home this evening.' It was a teasing rebuke, but nevertheless there was a steely edge to it. 'I'm Jarrett Hunter. And this is my wife, Abbie.' He put his arm affectionately about his wife's slender waist.

'Stazy Walker,' she returned lightly, allowing herself a smile at Jarrett's description of Jordan being his 'little brother'; there was nothing 'little' about Jordan, and the two men were of similar height. And, although she knew Jordan was the youngest of the three brothers, at the moment, grimly unsmiling as he was, he looked every one of the thirty-plus years she guessed him to be.

'Would you care to dance, Stazy Walker?' Jarrett invited smoothly.

'I was just about to ask her myself,' Jordan muttered—evoking a disbelieving look from Stazy as he did so.

He had been about to do no such thing; he'd already ignored her suggestion a few minutes ago that they dance! But he obviously wasn't happy with the thought of her dancing with his oldest brother—so unhappy about it he was even willing to escort her onto the floor himself in order to prevent it!

'Too late,' Jarrett replied lightly. 'Maybe next time,' he added tauntingly, a light but firm hand in the middle of Stazy's back as he guided her towards the other dancers. 'Why don't you invite my wife to dance?' he paused long enough to suggest to Jordan, before whirling Stazy away in time to the music.

Stazy loved to dance, and Jarrett Hunter was a more than capable partner, moving effortlessly in time to the music. But then, she had a feeling this man did most things well; his wife certainly looked contented enough as she and Jordan began to dance together a short distance away, the married couple sharing a glance of humour over Jordan's shoulder as he still scowled darkly.

Jordan was his own worst enemy, Stazy decided ruefully. He had obviously brought her here for a purpose, as a female partner for the evening, but one he could totally forget about once tonight was over. Behaving in the way that he was, Jordan was leaving himself open to the sort of mockery she was sure his brother Jarrett could dish out by the barrel-load. Not that she thought Jordan would appreciate her telling him as much; he was too immersed in himself—for whatever reason!—to listen to anyone, least of all her!

'Have you and Jordan known each other very long?'

Ouch. Stazy inwardly grimaced at Jarrett's casual question. It was obvious—to her, at least; Jordan didn't seem to have done too much thinking at all!—that Jordan's family were going to be very curious about the woman he had brought with him to this family wedding. And the Hunter family, from the little she had observed of them, did not appear to be backwards in coming forwards; Jarrett certainly hadn't been!

She wished she had realised earlier the curiosity her presence here was going to arouse. As early as yesterday, when Jordan had first invited her. Because if she had she wouldn't have accepted!

'A couple of months.' Stazy answered Jarrett evasively. She couldn't really tell Jordan's older brother that until yesterday Jordan had barely been aware of her existence! That didn't do her any favours, let alone Jordan. But, to be fair to herself, if she had realised she would be going to his brother's wedding reception, she would have made sure she had told him she was busy!

'Jordan is a little uptight at the moment,' Jarrett told her.

Stazy looked at him with raised brows. 'Only at the moment?'

Uptight was not the word she would have used to describe Jordan, but as she didn't intend meeting any of these people again—including Jordan himself, next-door neighbour or not!—she felt it would be as well if she kept her opinions to herself. Good-looking though he was, Jordan was still one of the rudest, most arrogant men she had ever met. And she had met more than her fair share of them!

'Weddings have this effect on him,' Jarrett explained laughingly. 'Especially family ones,' he added pointedly.

But his point was lost on Stazy. Unless her earlier guess about a love triangle was correct...?

'They can be—traumatic,' she said noncommittally.

'Are you Canadian or American?' Jarrett prompted interestedly at her obvious reluctance to respond to his questions.

Trying a different tack, Stazy realised, knowing she had been correct in her assessment of Jarrett being an astute and clever man. As the founder of Hunter's, a company dealing in hotels and property all over the world, and a director, along with his two brothers, he was unlikely to be anything else! Oh, well, she would play along with this game for a while—until it didn't suit her to do so any longer.

She smiled at Jarrett, blue eyes glowing with mischief. 'And until yesterday I had always thought my English education had obliterated most of my American accent!'

He raised dark brows. 'What happened yesterday to tell you otherwise?'

Jordan had spoken to her—really spoken to her, rather than offering the odd terse greeting—for the first time!

But she wouldn't tell Jarrett that. After the way he had behaved so far this evening, she certainly didn't owe Jordan any loyalty, and she was still more than a little annoyed with him for dropping her into this awkward situation with his brother in the first place, but her mother had always taught her that two wrongs did not make a right! She could cheerfully have kicked Jordan in the shin for abandoning her to his brother's mercy, and she would much prefer the physical satisfaction of administering that kick than getting back at him any other way!

'When I'm in England people tend to know I'm American,' she replied, effectively ignoring the probing in his question. 'But when I'm at home everyone assumes I'm English.' She gave a rueful shake of her head.

'Can't win, hmm?' Jarrett acknowledged understandingly. 'Might one ask why, when America has some damned fine schools of its own, you were educated in England?'

One might ask—but one wasn't about to get an answer! Not in any great detail, anyway. This man missed nothing, she realised, separating the waffle from what was really important. She had made a throw-away comment about her English education—but it was this fact Jarrett had latched onto. Because he knew by asking it he could learn much more about her background—and, hopefully, about her along with it.

She shrugged. 'Parents tend to make these decisions for their children, don't they?' she responded, looking curiously around the crowded room. 'Talking of parents—which lucky pair are your own parents?'

Jarrett's mouth twisted as the tables were turned on him. 'Our parents are divorced,' he rasped. 'But my father and stepmother are about somewhere,' he went on more lightly.

But not his mother... Interesting. Although Stazy could see by the slightly puzzled expression on Jarrett's face that he thought, if she and Jordan had been seeing each other for a couple of months, she would have known their parents were divorced...

Another oversight on Jordan's part. Again not her fault. She hadn't even known Jordan had one brother until this evening, let alone two.

'It happens.' She shrugged off the divorce. It did happen, as statistics showed all too often, and the fact that Jordan's mother wasn't present at her own son's wedding hinted at the fact that this one had been acrimonious. 'Personally, I think it's much better for people to part if they are unhappy, rather than try and make it work for the children. From what I've observed,' she continued, 'the kids usually end up more scarred than the parents!'

Jarrett's brow cleared. 'I hadn't thought of it in quite that way before...'

Because he was too close to the situation, Stazy guessed. Although it was odd that the three Hunter brothers had remained close to their father and not their mother. She wondered if—

No! She did not want to know anything about Jordan

or his family. She did not want to get involved. Tonight had been a mistake, and the further—and quicker—she removed herself from it the better!

'Are you—?'

'My dance, I believe, Jarrett,' Jordan told his older brother with satisfaction as he arrived at their side, Abbie Hunter giving Stazy a sympathetic smile as she accompanied him.

Stazy could imagine that while she and Jarrett had been chatting quite amiably Jordan had continued to be his taciturn self as he danced with Abbie. In fact, Jordan had probably spent the time wondering what she and Jarrett were finding to talk about!

'Mind he doesn't step on your toes, Stazy,' Jarrett warned mockingly as he led his wife away.

'Sarcasm is the lowest form of wit,' Jordan muttered as he and Stazy began to dance.

That was only the case if you didn't rise to it, Stazy thought ruefully. And in Jordan's case he rose all too easily to his brother's barbs.

'You dance very well,' Stazy told him, brightly, having no trouble at all following his steps, his hand light on her back.

Jordan looked down at her. 'You and Jarrett seemed to be getting on well together...?'

Predictable, or what! 'He was quite charming,' she said casually.

Jordan gave a disbelieving snort. 'Jarrett is the arrogant one in the family. And Jonathan is the charmer.'

Stazy raised auburn brows. 'Where does that leave you?' she returned quickly.

He frowned, seeming puzzled for a moment, and then he gave a smile. It transformed him, Stazy noted with dismay. It was a roguishly sexy smile, his eyes like molten gold, those laughter lines she had noted earlier beside his eyes and mouth were put to full use. Stazy felt a fluttering sensation in the pit of her stomach. Gone was the broodingly handsome man, and in his place was—

'Devilish,' Jordan told her, and Stazy was able to see the glittering humour in his eyes before he pulled her closer to him, both arms about her waist now as they danced to the seductively slow music. 'I haven't been very good company for you so far this evening, have I?' he murmured close to her ear. 'Let's see if we can improve on that.'

She didn't want him to improve on it! Taciturn would do her just fine. A devilish Jordan Hunter was not—

That face! She knew that man's face in the crowd of people talking across the room!

She stiffened in Jordan's arms, straining to see past the other dancers to where she had found that face she'd recognised. All she could see now was the back of the man's head; his face was turned away from her. But it couldn't have been him! Not here. She must have been mistaken.

'Hey, I'm only trying to apologise because I was a little preoccupied earlier,' Jordan chided softly as he obviously felt her tension. 'I'm not suggesting ravishing you on the dance floor!'

That might have been preferable to the shock she had just received. At least she could have dealt with that.

She couldn't stay here now. She had to leave. She couldn't possibly have seen the man she had thought she had—that person was far removed from the Hunter family—but it was enough that she had thought she recognised him.

She should never have accepted Jordan's invitation in the first place!

'I have to go, Jordan.' She pulled abruptly out of his arms, already searching for the exit.

Jordan looked stunned, frowning darkly once again. 'Stazy—'

'It's been lovely,' she told him distractedly—untruthfully! 'We must do this again some time,' she went on hurriedly, knowing she had no intention of seeing him again.

Escape! She had to get away!

Jordan's mouth twisted. 'I don't have any more brothers' weddings to invite you to!' he said sardonically, looking totally perplexed by her need to leave so soon.

Stazy barely glanced at him, having located the door now, and began threading her way through the people to reach it. If she could just—

'Stazy, what the hell are you doing?' Jordan caught up with her as she got out into the hallway, swinging her round to face him, his humour of a few minutes ago once again replaced by brooding intensity. 'I brought you here, I'll take you home again,' he stated harshly.

She understood his dilemma; his date walking out on him, quite so publicly, was the last thing he needed! But she couldn't help that; she simply couldn't stay here, felt too upset.

'You can't leave yet, Jordan.' She shook her head. 'But I—I have to go now!'

'I'll drive you home—'

'No!' she refused agitatedly. 'Now please let me go—'

'Having trouble, Jordan?' came a gently sarcastic female voice. 'And I always thought you had more luck with women than this.'

Jordan's hand left Stazy's arm as if she had stung him,

his face a furiously cold mask as he turned to look at the other woman who now stood in the corridor.

Stazy looked at her too, intrigued by the effect she had had on Jordan. Tiny and blonde, she was absolutely beautiful, her face as small and perfect as a doll's, dominated by huge brown eyes. Eyes that met Jordan's accusing gaze unflinchingly...

'What the hell are you doing here, Stella?' he ground out insultingly, every inch of his body taut.

Stazy groaned inwardly; if he ever looked at *her* in that disgusted way, she would want to shrivel up and die! As it was, desperate as she was to leave, she felt frozen to the spot, caught in a frozen tableau with these two people, one furiously angry, the other seeming completely unconcerned. In fact, the woman looked positively gleeful at Jordan's fury!

The woman lifted her shoulders carelessly, the perfection of her dainty figure shown to advantage by the black dress she wore. 'Where else would I be on Jonathan's wedding day?' she returned.

So she knew Jonathan too. This was all becoming too complicated for Stazy. And complications were things she was anxious to avoid at this time in her life. 'I really do have to go, Jordan.' She touched his arm to attract his attention; she had the distinct impression he had once again forgotten her existence! 'I'll catch up with you later,' she said in parting.

'Try leaving a shoe on the stairs on your way out,' the woman told her disparagingly. 'I'm told that usually works!' Her gaze was openly challenging as she looked Stazy up and down.

Stazy paused long enough to give her a narrow-eyed glance. Whoever she was, and whatever she meant to Jordan, or the charming Jonathan, Stazy certainly didn't

like this lady's implication that Stazy was Cinderella to
Jordan's Prince Charming!

She coldly returned the older woman's gaze. 'I'm
afraid I'm all out of glass slippers,' she responded
smartly. 'And I haven't kissed a prince yet that hasn't
turned into a frog! Have fun,' she told Jordan breezily
before turning and walking unhurriedly away, her head
held high.

CHAPTER TWO

JORDAN watched Stazy leave, really watched her, seeing her as more than just the beautiful redhead who lived next door to him, and whom he had only really noticed for the first time yesterday.

There was no doubt she was beautiful: those candid blue eyes, the sprinkling of freckles across the bridge of her tiny nose, her wide, smiling mouth. Or that she moved with the natural grace of her countrywomen, her legs long and shapely, her figure stunning in a fitted blue dress.

Those were the reasons he had chosen to invite Stazy Walker to accompany him here this evening. But he had just realised there was a lot more to her than surface beauty. A lot more...

'Don't tell me you're smitten, Jordan?' the woman at his side said disgustedly. 'The Hunter men are falling like flies!'

Jordan turned to Stella, his eyes as hard as the metal they resembled. 'And what does that have to do with you?' he said impatiently, all too aware of Stazy's comment 'I'll catch up with you later'; unfortunately, something much more immediate had his attention now. A pity he hadn't realised earlier that Stazy's temperament matched her long, fiery-red hair. Later, he promised himself.

'My darling boy—'

'I am not your "darling" anything,' he snarled, his expression contemptuous, completely unmoved by

Stella's kittenish looks; in her case, they were only skin-deep! Literally. As her favourite cosmetic surgeon knew only too well! Hell, she looked little older than he did, forty at the most, and yet of course she was much older than that... 'I suggest we get out of here.' He firmly grasped her arm as he closed the door behind him, turning her to leave. 'Before anyone else becomes aware of your presence.'

Stella stood her ground in the hallway. 'I'm not going anywhere, Jordan,' she resisted. 'I want to see Jonathan on his wedding day. And, of course, Jarrett—'

'Aren't you rather presuming that any of us want to see you?' Jarrett rasped harshly from behind them, having quietly left the reception room to join them. 'And in the circumstances that's presuming all too damned much! You're an uninvited guest, Stella,' he added coldly, looking down the length of his arrogant nose at her. 'I suggest you leave right now—before I have you thrown out!'

Jordan looked admiringly at his oldest brother. As usual, Jarrett wasn't pulling his punches. Stella now had an unattractive flush to her cheeks, her eyes glittering dangerously at Jarrett's insulting tone, meeting his gaze challengingly. But, nonetheless, Jordan was in no doubt who would win this particular battle of wills!

'You wouldn't do that, Jarrett.' Stella was finally the one to speak—and not as confidently as her words implied, either.

Jarrett's mouth thinned. 'Try me,' he returned softly, meeting her defiance unflinchingly.

'But I haven't even seen Jonathan yet,' Stella protested. 'Or met his bride—'

'And you aren't about to, either,' Jarrett bit back. 'In another couple of hours Jonathan and Gaye will leave the reception. So far they have had a perfect day; I don't intend letting you ruin it for them!'

'That's a very cruel thing to say to me, Jarrett. But then you always were unfeeling,' Stella told him emotionally.

As displays went, it was certainly a good one, Jordan acknowledged cynically; tears swam in those huge brown eyes, and her chin quivered ever so slightly in an effort to control herself. But Jordan knew as well as Jarrett did that it was all an act; Stella had never cared for anyone else in the whole of her life, and she was too damned old to change now—despite her cosmetic surgeon!

Jordan's mouth pursed contemptuously. 'Jarrett is right, Stella,' he said coldly. 'You aren't staying.'

He inwardly acknowledged he hadn't exactly been the life and soul of the party today himself—for which he probably owed Stazy an apology. No wonder she had decided to leave so abruptly; she had been as sick of his company as he was!

But he also knew that Stella's presence at the wedding reception was tantamount to introducing a cat amongst the pigeons. 'I'll take you wherever you want to go,' he offered. 'But you aren't staying here.'

'Oh, but I am,' Stella informed him confidently. 'Quite literally. I have a suite booked on the fourth floor!' she announced triumphantly.

Where she had no doubt waited out the first part of the evening before coming down here to make her entrance! For Jordan didn't doubt this whole thing had been premeditated, and he could see by Jarrett's narrowed eyes that he knew it too.

'What do you want, Stella?' Jarrett snapped impatiently.

Her head went back defensively. 'Why should you assume I want anything?'

Jarrett sighed. 'Because your sort always want something—'

'*My* sort!' she repeated in a voice rising with hysteria. 'How dare you? How dare you—?'

'Believe me, he dares,' Jordan told her dryly, still retaining that firm grasp of her arm; there was no way she was going to slip past both of them and make her entrance as planned. 'And so dare I. Let's go. Quietly,' he instructed firmly, aware that he and Jarrett couldn't remain out here for much longer before attracting attention to the fact they were both missing from the reception.

He didn't give Stella any more opportunity to argue with him, pulling her along beside him down the hallway and back into the main reception of the hotel.

She waited only that long before pulling her arm out of his grip, glaring up at him, her face set in an angry mask. 'You have no right, Jordan—'

'I have every right!' he returned icily. 'And so does Jarrett. Jonathan too, if he knew you were here.' He shook his head. 'I can't believe the nerve of you, just turning up here and expecting a welcome!'

'I am your mother!' she cried furiously.

He looked at her dispassionately. Yes, this woman had given birth to him. To Jarrett and Jonathan too. But his *mother*...?

He didn't think so! He had been fourteen when she'd walked out on him, his two older brothers, and her newly bankrupt husband. The previous years of his life had been filled with a long line of his mother's lovers, and her verbally violent rows with their cuckolded father. As for the loving and caring part of motherhood—! Jarrett and Jonathan had more or less brought him up, looked out for him, even before their mother left; in fact, he couldn't remember a single occasion when she had been there for him...

'Mother is only a word, Stella,' he said frigidly. 'And in your case it isn't even correct.'

He looked at her critically, her beauty, the slender figure, the fashionable clothes. None of it impressed him. He had seen this woman only once in the last twenty years, very briefly, after her second marriage had fallen apart and before she'd found husband number three. She had come to London to seek out her 'little boys', though at twenty-five, twenty-seven and twenty-nine they had hardly been that any more. If, indeed, they ever had been...

'What's happened, Stella?' he asked dryly. 'Has husband number three grown tired of you too?'

The angry flush that coloured her cheeks told him he had guessed correctly. It hadn't been too difficult; they might have no contact with her, but Jarrett, in his wisdom, kept a weather eye on her life—in the hopes of ensuring it never interfered with theirs!

Stella looked at him accusingly. 'You're becoming as hard and unfeeling as Jarrett!'

'We both had a good teacher,' he returned hardly.

Stazy should be back at her apartment by now. If he could get away from Stella, return to the reception and make his excuses to Jonathan and Gaye, he might just be in time to call on Stazy before she went to bed...

Stazy in bed... That lithe, silken body naked, her only adornment her long flaming red hair...

Now there was something worth seeing. How ever could he not have noticed what a stirringly beautiful and desirable woman Stazy was?

He had been acting like a complete idiot all evening,

scowling at everyone, barely speaking, and paying absolutely no attention to the woman he had brought with him. No wonder Stazy had walked out on him. What a fool he was! He might have sworn off marriage, but not women. There had been a beautiful female living next door to him for three months, and he hadn't even noticed. Get your act together, Jordan, he remonstrated with himself. Stazy must think he was—

'Why are you smiling?' the woman who had given birth to him thirty-five years ago demanded indignantly. 'This isn't in the least bit funny—'

'I couldn't agree more, Mother.' His mouth twisted derisively at the way she flinched at the name; a woman trying to look thirty-five did not want to be reminded she had a son of that age—and two more even older than that! 'This situation isn't funny, but *you* are hilarious. You want something, Stella, and we all know it, so I suggest you stop playing games and get to the point. But a word of advice: don't use Jonathan's wedding as a way to get what you want from Jarrett. You would regret it!'

'Don't threaten me, Jordan,' she warned, her face pale now, set in harsh lines.

He shook his head wearily. 'I said it was advice, and that's exactly what it was. Go ahead and gatecrash the wedding.' He waved invitingly towards the hallway leading to the reception room. 'You'll find yourself marched out of there again so fast you'll wonder what happened to you! You think I'm becoming hard and unfeeling? Push Jarrett some more and see what happens. And heaven help you—because no one else will!'

She met his gaze for several seconds, and then she wavered, before dropping her eyes away completely, as she obviously rethought her game-plan.

Because this was a game to her, Jordan knew. She had been playing one game or another with them all her life. Playing mother had lasted long enough for her to produce the three boys, and for their father's money to run out. Then she had run off looking for another game to play. And, as Jordan had guessed earlier, this sudden urge to be 'Mother' again had something to do with her third marriage. Without a rich husband to support her she couldn't maintain her lavish lifestyle. She needed money for that, and in the last twenty years her three sons had managed to amass quite a lot of that!

With a mother like her was it any wonder he was a cynic where women were concerned?

'I really don't have any more time to waste standing here talking to you, Stella,' he told her hardly before turning away.

'Running after Cinderella?' she called after him tauntingly.

Jordan turned slowly back to face the woman he had once known as Mummy, feeling absolutely nothing towards her now. Not even hate, he realised. She was just a very sad woman, trying desperately to cling onto the things that mattered to her—her looks and the money to keep them. Outwardly she was beautiful, inwardly she was ugly. And there was nothing that plastic surgery could do to change that!

'I've never run after a woman in my life,' he replied before going back down the hallway to the reception.

He wasn't 'running after' Stazy; after he had made the appropriate excuses to Jonathan and Gaye, he was simply going home. Stazy just happened to live in the apartment next door to his!

And who knew? Maybe tonight would be the night

Stazy would kiss a prince and he wouldn't turn into a frog…

She was a long time answering his ring on the doorbell. Probably she was surprised to hear the internal doorbell and not the entryphone. But she was certainly worth waiting for when she did finally open the door, having changed out of the blue dress into a pair of figure-hugging blue denims and a skimpy blue top, her hair—beautiful, gloriously red hair, like a Renaissance paint-ing—falling the length of her spine like a moving flame. And the freckles on her nose seemed more pro-nounced—and more endearing.

'Jordan?' She looked taken aback to see him standing there.

'You didn't have any champagne earlier.' He smiled, holding up the cooled bottle of bubbly liquid and two glasses, that he had taken from the wedding reception on his way out. 'An oversight I felt needed rectifying,' he added huskily. It had been his own morose temper earlier that had created the 'oversight'; he hadn't even given her the common courtesy then of ensuring she was provided with a drink!

Her eyes widened, the deepest, clearest blue he had ever seen. 'Wouldn't you rather be sharing that with Stella?' she queried, making no effort to open the door wider and move aside so that he could enter her apart-ment.

Not that he could blame her for that, either; he hadn't exactly been attentive so far in their acquaintance. And from the cool way she was looking at him, he wasn't sure he was going to be given the chance to make amends!

'Stella is something else that needs rectifying,' he drawled dismissively.

'You don't owe me any explanations, Jordan—'

'I know that,' he replied sharply. He didn't owe any woman anything! 'I just thought it would be nice if we shared some champagne together,' he continued less aggressively—so much for making a fresh start with Stazy!

'Okay,' she accepted without further argument, opening the door to let him in.

Jordan was a little taken aback at her sudden acquiescence, but he stepped inside before she changed her mind as quickly.

Her apartment had the same layout as his own; he knew that because he had looked at it first when he was thinking of moving in five years ago, but in the end had decided that the apartment he had now possessed the better view of the two.

But as soon as he stepped inside he could see the differences in their tastes. Stazy had chosen decor in creams and golds, with bright splashes of orange, giving a much lighter, airier feel, a warmth, that his own green, cream and brown furnishings didn't achieve.

The touches of orange in the rugs and scatter cushions somehow seemed to be the same shade of burnt copper as her hair, the furniture in the lounge she took him into consisting mainly of big, comfortable-looking armchairs and several huge bean-bags. Overall, Jordan felt a peace and restfulness amongst this casual comfort that he didn't feel in his own apartment.

'This is great,' he told Stazy admiringly, putting the bottle of champagne and glasses down on a very low table. 'You'll have to give me the name of your interior designer.'

'Stazy Walker,' she provided softly.

His brows rose. 'You decorated all of this yourself?'

Stazy nodded, smiling slightly at his obvious amazement. 'I'm an interior designer.'

He gave the sitting room another look. She was good. Very good. And his apartment hadn't been decorated since he'd moved in... Not that he spent a great deal of time there anyway, being either out at work, or just out. But if she could transform her own apartment in this way...

He picked up the bottle of champagne. 'I don't suppose you would be interested in a job?'

Stazy curled herself up on one of the bean-bags while he uncorked the champagne, and she eyed him warily across the room. 'Doing what?' she prompted guardedly.

Now that he had taken the trouble to notice her at all, Stazy Walker was fast becoming an enigma to him! She had seemed so open and friendly, but with each thing she revealed about herself she appeared to be holding something else back... In fact, he knew absolutely nothing of real relevance about her, he realised with a start. Like what she was doing in England at all. Where were her family? If she had any family.

'Decorating my apartment,' he told her, pouring out the champagne before handing her one of the glasses. 'What did you think I meant?'

'You wouldn't believe some of the suggestions I've had over the last three months!' she told him disgustedly.

Jordan settled himself down in one of the comfortable armchairs, finding it as soft and bolstered as it looked; the bean-bags looked relaxing to sprawl in, but the last thing he wanted was to get down on one of those things and then struggle to get back up onto his feet when the time came! He had to be a good twelve, or maybe four-

teen years older than the age he guessed Stazy to be, but
he didn't have to end up on a bean-bag looking decrepit!

'Try me,' he invited, his curiosity piqued.

She shrugged. 'Maybe it has something to do with the
language—we do speak a different language, no matter
what anyone tries to say to the contrary. When I first
moved here I got a job as a window-dresser in one of
the large stores in town—I'd rather not say which one!'
She grimaced. 'The manager's idea of working after the
store was closed was to try and drag me off to the bed
department, to see if there were any improvements I
could make there!'

Jordan was having trouble holding back a smile at the
graphic picture she portrayed—and he certainly didn't
think it had anything to do with a language problem;
Stazy was beautiful, whatever language she spoke!

'What happened?' he asked.

'I kneed him in the place I felt needed improving,'
she told him directly. 'I also got fired,' she sighed. 'For
being unsuitable for the job! Actually, I've always preferred working in people's homes, so after that I put a
few cards in shop windows, hoping to get some business
that way. I was offered a job decorating a little boy's
bedroom.'

'Sounds safe enough,' Jordan drawled—because he
had a feeling it hadn't been safe at all.

Stazy grimaced again. 'That "little boy" turned out
to be about sixty-five—and he wanted me to do the decorating wearing a gym-slip!'

This was just too much for Jordan, unable to hold
back his chuckles any longer. In fact, he more than
chuckled; he couldn't help it. 'What sort of shop windows did you put your cards in?' he finally sobered
enough to query.

'You're much quicker than me!' Stazy gave him a shy grin. 'I realised that had been my mistake when the next "client" who rang asked me my age, and told me to bring along a set of red underwear!'

'I prefer cream myself,' Jordan observed.

'I took all my cards back before I got any more calls like that!' She shook her head disgustedly. 'Do you suppose people actually enjoy that sort of thing? Telephoning a complete stranger for sex?' She grimaced her distaste at the idea.

Jordan looked at her. She couldn't be that innocent. Could she...? 'How old are you, Stazy?' he mused.

'Twenty-one, almost twenty-two,' she supplied promptly, her tone implying she didn't see what that had to do with anything.

She was young. Younger than any of the women he had been involved with in recent years—though he wasn't going to get involved with Stazy Walker; he was just curious, that was all.

'Don't you read the newspapers?' There was an edge of scorn to his voice, created by that residual anger towards himself.

She stood up in one gracefully fluid movement, her glass steady in her hand. 'Of course I read the newspapers,' she returned impatiently. 'But to find a bed-partner in such a way seems— What work do you want done on your apartment?' She abruptly changed the subject. 'Which room?'

'All of them,' he decided, relaxing back in his chair. 'Are you up to it, do you think?' he derided.

She looked ready to tell him what he could do with his offer of work. But something held her back, and she turned away, breathing deeply.

Jordan accepted she hadn't had a very good time of

it since moving to London. And he wasn't helping to make it any better. Besides, this apartment, as he knew only too well, was expensive to rent. And with no visible means of income— He wasn't a charity, damn it!

'Are you?' he pressed harshly at her continued silence.

She whipped quickly round to face him, two bright spots of angry colour in her cheeks. 'My work speaks for itself,' she bit out tautly.

Jordan had the distinct impression she wanted to tell him—and his offer of work—to go to hell. But she wasn't going to do so. Again, something held her back...

'It does.' He nodded in agreement. 'You'll need to see the apartment, of course—'

'Isn't it exactly the same as this one?' She sipped her champagne now, looking at him over the glass's rim.

Those eyes. So clear a blue. Like a Canadian mountain lake he had once seen. And this girl/woman was as fresh as that mountain lake...

Jordan shook his head to rid it of those thoughts. He was offering her work, for goodness' sake! 'Exactly like this one,' he confirmed tersely. 'When can you start?'

She raised her palms in a gesture of resistance. 'I'll need ideas from you before I start to put anything together—'

'I thought interior designers were the ones with the ideas,' he cut in. 'Isn't that the reason they're the interior designers? Don't you present me with ideas, we discuss them—and then you get on and do exactly what you want to do?'

Those blue eyes narrowed at what had been his deliberately derisive tone. 'Jordan, I have a feeling you're playing games with me—'

'I never play when it comes to business, Stazy,' he

assured her softly. 'You—' He broke off as the security intercom buzzed; downstairs someone needed admittance. And then it sounded again. 'Hadn't you better answer that?' he prompted Stazy as she made no effort to do so.

She still did not move. 'Obviously someone has made a mistake; I don't know anyone in London.'

Then it was strange that she had come to live here, Jordan could have said. But didn't. It was part of the enigma that was Stazy Walker, he decided. Best not to get too involved.

'Perhaps it's the little boy with your gym-slip?' he suggested sardonically. 'I think you should answer it, Stazy,' he said as the intercom buzzed once more, putting down his empty champagne glass. This evening hadn't turned out quite as he would initially have liked it to, but maybe it was better this way. 'If only to tell the person to go away,' he said as the intercom buzzed again—and this time went on buzzing; the person was obviously keeping their finger on the button. 'They're very persistent for someone who has made a mistake,' he murmured interestedly.

Stazy claimed she knew no one in England, and so it followed that no one should know her either, but the names of the people occupying the apartments were clearly marked beside the entryphone buttons downstairs; it was very unlikely someone had got the wrong apartment. Yet Stazy still seemed reluctant to acknowledge that intercom...

'Would you like me to—?'

'No!' She hastily cut off his offer, putting down her glass and moving towards the entryphone—which all the occupants of the apartments had.

His entryphone had saved Jordan several times in the

past, when he had a woman in his apartment with him and another one was downstairs calling to come up; it was much easier to make excuses to the woman he was with when she couldn't hear the other end of the conversation!

That Stazy didn't even want him to hear her replies in the conversation which followed was obvious as she looked at him pointedly, obviously wanting him to leave before she answered the call.

Jordan's answer was to stroll over to the window, his back turned towards her, but he was completely aware of what was happening in the room behind him, Stazy's reflection on the window in front of him. She was glaring at him, seemed deeply irritated with him. But she had piqued his interest now; he had no intention of leaving until she had answered that call. Besides, they hadn't yet finished discussing the work she was going to do for him...

'Yes?' Stazy spoke agitatedly behind him into the receiver. 'What are *you* doing here?' she demanded exasperatedly. 'No, you can't! Zak, I said no,' she added more firmly. 'I'm not even going to ask how you found me, I'm just telling you to forget it again—' There was a slight pause, while Zak obviously argued his case. 'Zak, I don't care if you have nowhere else to stay. You can sleep on the streets for all I care—but you aren't staying here!' She slammed down the receiver, her uneven breathing easily heard in the otherwise silent room.

Jordan kept his gaze focused out of the window, although he was looking at none of the beauty of London at night lit up by hundreds of lights; his attention was all inwards. Stazy had said she knew no one in London, and yet she obviously knew this man Zak. Well enough, from what Jordan had gathered from the conversation, for the other man to think he could stay here in her apartment with her!

Who—or what—was this Zak to Stazy?

CHAPTER THREE

STAZY glanced across the room to where Jordan stood so still and quiet in front of her window. What on earth must he be thinking? She had just finished telling him of some of the ridiculous situations she had found herself in since her move here, and now she had some man calling up from downstairs asking if he could stay in her apartment with her! And Jordan had just offered her a job, too...!

Damn Zak. He had no right to just turn up here un-invited like this. He—

She jumped nervously as her doorbell rang. It was too much of a coincidence, too soon after Zak's call from downstairs...

How had he got into the apartment building? Because she didn't doubt that it was him standing outside her front door. Or that he wouldn't go away again until she had answered it!

As Jordan turned around, dark brows raised questioningly, she knew he wasn't going to leave just yet, either. Men!

'Do you want me to answer it?' Jordan offered smoothly. 'I could always send him on his way for you,' he offered.

She didn't doubt that he would try. Or that Zak would resist. Wonderful, just what she needed—a fight on her doorstep! Somehow she didn't think so; she had come back to England in the first place to get away from all of that.

She shook her head. 'I'll go. But I definitely think the security here needs looking into,' she said before striding off to answer the door.

This hadn't been a good evening so far, and with Zak's arrival it was deteriorating rapidly. Still, she supposed she and Jordan were about even in the complication stakes; that woman Stella had turned up in his life earlier—although his arrival here a short time ago seemed to imply she had been rapidly despatched again!—then there had been the man she'd recognised at his brother's wedding, and now Zak had arrived! How had he found out where she was living...?

Zak grinned at her confidently when she opened the door; tall, blond, with laughing blue eyes, he looked completely unabashed by his intrusion. 'Stazy!' His joyful cry was accompanied by his dropping his suitcase in order to pick her up in a bear-hug and swing her round in the hallway.

It was very difficult to remain angry with someone who looked so pleased to see her, and who could lift her up in his arms so easily she might have been a child!

Stazy gave him a rueful grin. 'Put me down, you clown.' She punched him playfully on the shoulder. 'And then could you explain to me exactly how you got up here?' she added reprovingly, sure that it hadn't been done legitimately. 'Please don't say you used the elevator!' She was fully aware of just how aggravating this man could be.

'Okay, Staze.' He put her down, still grinning, his American accent much more noticeable than her own. 'It was really easy.' He bent down to pick up the suitcase. 'I pressed the button for Apartment 4, told the lady that answered that I was the guy in Apartment 7, J. Hunter, and that I had forgotten my key to get into the building. It worked.' He shrugged. 'I saw it in a movie once.' He grinned his satisfaction at his success, having followed Stazy through to the sitting room as he gave his explanation. 'I didn't— Uh-oh, am I interrupting something?' He came to a halt as he spotted Jordan standing near the window, and the bottle of champagne and two glasses still on the table.

Stazy could see exactly the thoughts that were going through Zak's head—and probably so could Jordan. But Zak couldn't have been further from the truth, no matter how damning the evidence!

Jordan stepped forward, holding out his hand in greeting to Zak. 'J. Hunter,' he introduced dryly. 'The ''guy in Apartment 7'',' he tacked on deliberately so that there would be no mistake on Zak's part. 'And the J stands for Jordan,' he supplied.

The two men were of similar age, similar height too, but there the similarity ended; Zak brimmed over with boyish good humour, while Jordan was much more reserved as the two men shook hands.

'Sorry about that.' Zak grinned unrepentantly. 'But Stazy can be damned awkward when she wants to be,' he said affectionately.

'The word is private, Zak,' she put in before Jordan could add anything to that—one way or the other! 'Jordan Hunter, meet Zak Prince. And vice versa.' She resented having to make this introduction at all. One—or both!—of these men had to leave! But one looked like being her employer for the foreseeable future, and the other one—! That suitcase Zak had brought in with him looked distinctly ominous!

'Prince.' Jordan repeated the name slowly, his expression thoughtful as he looked at Stazy.

She watched him warily. What was he thinking? Did he know—? Had he realised—?

He turned to Zak. 'We were discussing the merits— or otherwise—of princes earlier,' he explained. 'The fairy-tale kind,' he amended softly.

Stazy had said she hadn't kissed a prince yet that hadn't turned into a frog! Well, it was true—literally— Zak was chief frog!

'Need I say more?' She looked irritatedly at the blond giant who had invaded her apartment so effectively.

Jordan smiled at the joke. 'I'm sure you have a lot more to say to this particular Prince,' he drawled. 'And that you would probably prefer to say it when I'm not around! Tomorrow is Sunday,' he continued considering ly. 'Will you be able to start work on Monday?'

She blinked at his directness. Of course she could start on Monday—her diary wasn't exactly overflowing with work, as she had already told him. But—

'Get some ideas together,' Jordan ordered as he walked confidently to the door. 'And we'll discuss them Monday evening when I get back from work.' He glanced across at Zak as the other man made himself comfortable on one of the bean-bags before sitting forward to top up the champagne for himself in one of the glasses. 'At my apartment,' Jordan stated hardly. 'I'll expect you around seven-thirty.'

Stazy walked with him to the door. 'I'm sorry about Zak,' she said awkwardly. 'I— He—'

'You don't owe me any explanations, either, Stazy,' He reminded her of her own comment to him earlier in the evening.

Of course she didn't. This was business, after all. Although a part of her suspected that hadn't been Jordan's intention when he'd come to her apartment half an hour ago! Perhaps it was as well Zak had arrived when he did...

'Seven-thirty Monday evening,' she acknowledged briskly, closing the door firmly behind Jordan once he had left.

Now she must go and tackle Zak. Because he wasn't staying here. No matter what sort of persuasion he might try to use!

'Zak, will you get out of that bathroom *right now*!' Stazy banged loudly on the bathroom door in accompaniment to her demand. 'I've been waiting almost an hour to take my shower,' she cried furiously.

'Calm down, Stazy,' he soothed in a completely un-ruffled voice. 'You aren't due at Jordan's for another half an hour yet.'

So much for making Zak leave, she told herself. As she had known he would from the onset, Zak had whee-dled his way into persuading her to let him stay, just until he got fixed up with a hotel. Which, as Stazy knew only too well, would probably never materialise; Zak liked his home comforts, someone always there—usually for him!

Stazy had made it clear that his 'someone' wasn't go-ing to be her; if he was staying in England for any length of time, at her apartment, then he could do his share of the chores and cooking. His share of the cooking yes-terday had comprised taking her to the nearest fast-food restaurant for Sunday lunch, assuring her that she could have the chicken or the ribs when she'd protested she didn't even like burgers. As a change it had been fine, but as a staple diet—Zak's staple diet, if left to his own devices!—it just wasn't good enough.

'Move it, Zak,' she told him in a strained tone. The

last thing she needed was to be stressed out when she went to see Jordan. Besides, it was her bathroom!

Apart from getting to know her in her apartment, Jordan hadn't seen her doing business yet, and she wanted to make a good impression. He might have reconsidered things since Saturday, and decided he didn't want his place redecorated after all...

'I mean it, Zak.' She rattled the door handle impatiently. This was worse than when she had lived at home and had to fight her three brothers for the use of one of the two bathrooms. 'If you aren't out of there by the time I count to five, you can start looking for somewhere else—' She broke of her tirade as the bathroom door was opened from the inside, and Zak stood there enveloped in a cloud of steam, with one towel draped about his neck, and another one—thank goodness!—draped about his waist and thighs. 'I hope you haven't used all the hot water,' she grumbled as she strode past him into the now overheated bathroom. 'Zak—!' she gasped as she looked around.

'I'll clear the mess up later,' he hastily assured her at her dismayed wail. 'You aren't the only one with somewhere to go this evening, you know,' he defended as she turned to glare at him angrily.

'Spare me the details,' she snapped. 'Just go away and leave me to—' She broke off as the doorbell rang.

'I'll get it,' Zak told her hurriedly, obviously glad of the excuse to escape. 'You just carry on with your shower.'

He had gone before Stazy had time to stop him. And it had been the internal bell. Which could only mean one person... Jordan had changed his mind about the decorating. Damn it. She needed that job. She certainly wasn't about to crawl back home, having failed in what she set out to do. It was—

'Jordan,' Zak told her with a grin as he strolled back down the hallway, using the towel that had been draped about his neck to dry off his hair after his fifteen-minute shower.

'Well?' Stazy finally said when the tension of waiting for him to continue became too much for her; she had known it was Jordan, but what did he want?

Zak blinked innocent blue eyes. 'I thought you were in a hurry to take your shower?'

'I am,' she ground out between gritted teeth. 'What did Jordan want?' As if she couldn't guess.

She had regaled him on Saturday with those two tales of confusion concerning her profession, and now Zak had answered the door to him wearing only a towel— two towels, to be exact. Jordan probably thought she was a high-class call-girl!

'Oh, that,' Zak replied, unconcerned. 'He said could you make it seven forty-five instead of seven-thirty? He's only just got in from work, and he would like to take a shower.'

Jordan hadn't changed his mind. Well, until Zak had opened the door to him a couple of minutes ago, wearing only a couple of towels, he hadn't...

'He isn't the only one,' she told Zak determinedly, grabbing the towel draped about his neck. 'See you later.' She closed the bathroom door firmly in his face.

A lot later, she hoped. With any luck Zak would have left for wherever he was going by the time she finished her own shower, leaving her to get ready to face Jordan in peace and quiet.

Quiet. It was something she had learnt to value the last three months. At home there had always been so much going on, people constantly around. But since she had moved here she had become used to doing what she wanted, when she wanted, and that included whether or not she spent time with others!

Though it had been the desire to be around people that had involved her in Jordan Hunter's life on Saturday…!

But she had won herself a job from that. At least, she hoped she had.

It was seven forty-five exactly when Stazy rang the door-bell of the apartment next door. And she was, she hoped, dressed for the part, her pale blue blouse tucked neatly into the waistband of navy blue striped trousers. Businesslike, but the fitted style of the blouse and trousers was also feminine. After all, Saturday evening when she'd worn the clinging blue dress she had been out on a date; this evening was work.

Although she wasn't too sure of that once Jordan had opened the door and invited her in, and she saw the dining-table set for two, with candles flickering on it, the other lighting in the room subdued.

'I thought we could eat first,' Jordan told her lightly as she frowned across the table. 'Unless you've already eaten?' he enquired at her dismayed expression.

No, she hadn't already eaten, had been too nervous. She'd thought she would make herself a sandwich or something after she got back. Food was something else she didn't have to worry about too much now that she lived on her own; there were no rigid times for meals any more, there was no one else to answer to…

She might not have eaten yet this evening, but sitting down to a candlelit meal with Jordan Hunter was hardly businesslike! Especially as he looked more handsome than ever tonight, wearing a black shirt and fitted denims.

'Don't look so worried,' he teased. 'This isn't another variation of the little boy and his bedroom theme! And I can see for myself that you aren't wearing red underwear!' Those golden eyes looked at her assessingly.

Stazy looked down self-consciously at her blouse. It was made of silky material, not exactly see-through, but a red bra would certainly be visible through the light-coloured material. And Jordan had taken the time to notice that fact in the two minutes since she'd entered his apartment!

That and the candlelit dinner were what bothered her.

Jordan laughed softly as she still looked reluctant. 'It's just a Chinese takeaway,' he admitted. 'I'll blow out the candles and turn up the lights if you would feel more comfortable?'

She was being silly. It *was* only a meal. And they could discuss some of her ideas as they ate. 'No, this is fine,' she told him briskly, putting down the list of ideas she had brought in with her. 'I'll help you serve the food.'

It wasn't 'just' a takeaway as Stazy knew it: chicken noodle soup first, followed by three Chinese meat dishes, with bamboo shoots and rice, and to follow there was sticky-toffee bananas and apples. Jordan opened a bottle of deliciously cool, crisp white wine to go with it.

'I'm too full to work now I've finished this,' Stazy warned Jordan as he made them coffee.

He sat back down in the chair opposite hers. 'I owe you an apology for Saturday evening. I behaved very badly—'

'Of course you didn't,' Stazy protested. 'I had a good time.'

'Is that why you left so suddenly?' Jordan returned quickly. 'Because you were having such a good time?

No, that had been for another reason completely. She had thought back to Saturday evening a couple of times during yesterday and today, and she had almost decided she must have been mistaken about the man she had thought she'd seen at the reception. Almost...

'Jarrett explained to me that marriages tend to make you uptight,' she replied easily.

'Did he indeed?' Jordan murmured dryly. 'I see you have a house-guest,' he added softly.

He caught her completely off-guard with this sudden change of subject!

She had been in the process of sipping her coffee, but she almost choked on it at that moment. She certainly didn't need to ask whom Jordan was referring to!

'Zak can be hard to get rid of,' she acknowledged frankly.

'He seems quite likeable,' Jordan said, that golden gaze compelling as it held hers. 'Have you known him very long?'

'Quite some time, yes,' she answered guardedly. This conversation was going to lead nowhere—she would make sure of that! 'You haven't opened your fortune-cookie,' she encouraged brightly. 'Mine says, "Life will only look up if you do,"' she read out wryly.

She watched Jordan as he picked up his own cookie and broke it in half, slowly unfolding the piece of paper inside. It was all nonsense, of course, Stazy decided; she could just as easily have picked up the one Jordan had. And yet, perhaps life was starting to look up...

'"Love is like a balloon,"' Jordan read with a cynical smile. '"You must blow fresh air into it to make it lighter."'

Stazy laughed softly, standing up. 'So now you know!' She began to clear the plates away.

Jordan sat back in his chair, watching her. 'Time to get down to work?' he guessed.

'Time to get down to work,' she confirmed briskly.

And for the next half an hour that was exactly what they did. For all that Jordan had seemed so casual about this on Saturday, he knew what he liked and didn't like, and within a very short time they had, between them, agreed on some very workable ideas for the living room. In fact, Stazy felt quite excited at the thought of getting started.

'You'll need a key to let yourself in, of course,' Jordan ventured thoughtfully. 'I'll be at work during the day, and that's when you'll be able to get on with the redecoration,' he explained at her questioning look.

Of course she would. In normal circumstances, she wouldn't have thought anything of being offered the key to a client's home. Some of the people she had worked for in the States had actually moved out while she worked on their homes. But somehow, with Jordan, it didn't quite feel right.

'That's true,' she accepted tightly. 'And, contrary to what was said on Saturday, I'll check everything with you first before going ahead with it.'

He laughed, also standing up, stretching comfortably. 'Hit a raw nerve, did I?' he queried. 'I didn't mean to. But I think I also told you on Saturday that I prefer cream underwear to red!'

Stazy gave him a startled look. She *was* wearing cream underwear. And, from his expression, Jordan was well aware of that...! He didn't think she had worn it on purpose—!

'Jordan—'

'Stazy,' he returned huskily, reaching out to pull her into his arms. 'You're very beautiful, Stazy,' he told her throatily.

And he was very attractive, even more so after having spent the last couple of hours in his relaxed company. But *she* wasn't relaxed any more. 'Jordan, this is not a good idea—' she managed to protest—seconds before his lips came down on hers.

Damn whether or not this was a good idea—it felt wonderful! Jordan sipped at and tasted her lips, completely unhurried, his breath warm against her cheek, his arms enfolding her into the hard strength of his body, his hands lightly caressing her back.

This wasn't a great idea, Stazy knew that it wasn't, but it felt so good; her senses were spinning, her head along with them. Or maybe that was the wine they had consumed with their meal? Although she didn't think so...

His hair, thick and dark, felt so silky beneath her fingertips. And still he kissed her, that kiss deepening as passion surged between them and took over. Jordan's hands lightly covered her breasts, his tongue teasing an erotic pattern across her lower lip. He—

'Stop now, Jordan!' Stazy pulled away from him, her cheeks flushed, her breathing erratic. She swallowed hard, forcing herself to meet his questioning gaze. 'I'm sure one of your brothers—or possibly both of them!—has told you never to mix business with pleasure!'

He didn't move, only that slight tensing of his jaw showing he wasn't as unmoved by the kisses they had just shared as he would like to appear. 'Probably,' he acknowledged dismissively. 'Prince or frog, Stazy?' he said.

It took her a couple of seconds to realise what he

meant, and then her eyes narrowed disbelievingly. 'Is that the reason you kissed me?' she said disgustedly. 'To see if you could change my mind?'

Jordan shrugged lightly. 'You really shouldn't throw out those sort of challenges.'

It hadn't been a challenge, but a statement of fact. And this man had done nothing—with his last taunting question—to make her think any differently! Kissing her just to try and prove a point—! And she had responded. That was what angered her the most!

'I'll remember that in future,' she said tersely, collecting up her notes. 'I'll get back to you on the curtain fabric as soon as I can.' She headed determinedly for the door, anxious to leave.

'Going back to your Prince?' Jordan called after her.

She turned back sharply, blue eyes still flashing angrily. 'Don't be misled by the name, Jordan—he's a frog!'

Jordan's mouth twisted derisively. 'I thought you were going to say "He's just a man"!' he taunted.

Stazy gave a snort. 'And so he is,' she snapped, glad to have something to focus her anger on. Because she *was* angry—with herself. For a brief time—a very brief time!—she had thought Jordan might actually be different. Until he had immediately proved that he wasn't. How stupid could she be?

Jordan looked across at her with narrowed eyes. 'You're very young to be this cynical about men.'

She glared at him, continuing to be annoyed with herself for allowing Jordan to kiss her—and for kissing him back! 'I have no illusions where men are concerned, if that's what you mean,' she bit out scornfully—and even less so after this evening's fiasco! 'I learnt at a young age just how fickle your sex can be.'

Jordan gave her a considering look. 'Your father walked out on your mother,' he surmised shrewdly.

He hadn't exactly walked out—because he had never actually walked in!

Jordan was philosophical. 'It happens, Stazy,' he said carelessly. 'My mother walked out on my father too.'

And her three sons, Stazy realised, at last knowing why it was that their father had been at Jonathan's wedding but not, as far as she knew, their mother... What sort of woman left her husband with three sons to bring up on his own...?

'Consequently you have exactly the same distrust of women that I have of men,' she pointed out coolly.

'I suppose I do,' he accepted emotionlessly.

There was no 'suppose' about it. Stazy could also guess now why weddings made Jordan uptight, as Jarrett had described it. The Hunter men had obviously all stayed single well into their thirties, Jordan's older brothers both marrying only in the last couple of years, which must have come as a bit of a blow to him...

No wonder Jordan had chosen to take a complete stranger to Jonathan's wedding—he hadn't wanted any speculation concerning his own marital intentions. Because they didn't, and never would, exist!

Stazy grinned, her ill humour of a few minutes ago rapidly dispersing. She never had been able to stay angry for long. 'Nice to know we have something in common! I'll catch up with you later, Jordan.' She let herself out.

She was humming almost happily to herself as she let herself into her own apartment, but came to an abrupt halt when she opened the door to be met by loud music playing, and the smell of food cooking. Those two things were bad enough in themselves, but when she followed that smell of food into the kitchen—naturally!—it was to find Zak wasn't alone. The person sitting there with him was no more welcome than he was!

The two men at the breakfast bar were eating what looked to be bacon and eggs—looked to be, because Stazy was sure there hadn't been either in her refrigerator when she'd left earlier! So Zak was even buying his own food to cook in her kitchen. And he had made a damn mess while he was doing it; pots and pans covered most of the work surfaces, all still dirty, of course.

Stazy slammed her notes down on the one clean worktop. 'What are *you* doing here, Rik?' she demanded to know.

'Don't worry about it,' Zak assured his younger companion as he grimaced his surprise at her attack. 'She greeted me in the same way,' he explained offhandedly, standing up. 'Surprise, Stazy!' He grinned at her unabashedly. 'That's why I was in a hurry to get out this evening; I went to pick Rik up from the airport,' he told her cheerfully.

Stazy ignored the little-boy smile that went with the words, glaring at the younger man. 'You aren't staying, Rik,' she told him firmly. 'And neither are you,' she said to Zak.

'Stazy…?' Rik looked questioningly at Zak. He was as tall as the other man, but dark-haired, aged in his early thirties, dressed in his usual casual style of denims with a dark blue shirt, his rakish looks unquestionably handsome.

Zak seemed unconcerned. 'It was the name on the doorbell downstairs when I arrived, so I—'

'It's my name,' Stazy cut in impatiently. 'You two can be part of a comedy act if you want to, but I've opted out.' She turned furiously back to Rik. 'I suppose it's too much to hope that you might be booked into a hotel?' But she already knew the answer to that; Zak would have told him there was plenty of room here for him to stay!

Rik looked unperturbed by her anger, still seated at the breakfast bar, seeming perfectly comfortable and at home. But then, he would. As she knew from experience, these two could turn a palace into a pigsty within a few hours!

'This apartment seems quite big for just one person,' Rik said questioningly.

'I like it that way,' Stazy responded tautly. 'You can share Zak's bedroom tonight—but tomorrow you both move out,' she told them heatedly. 'After you've cleaned up the mess you've made.'

Her kitchen had been neat and tidy when she'd left earlier tonight; now it was almost unrecognisable. She shook her head disgustedly. How could they possibly have used so many pans, just to cook bacon and eggs?

'Bad evening, Staze?' Zak asked airily. 'I'm surprised. Jordan seemed quite interested.'

'My evening was just fine, thank you, Zak,' she snipped, not liking the speculation in his tone—but not about to answer it, either!

'Who's Jordan?' Rik prompted interestedly.

'He—'

'Someone I'm doing some work for.' Stazy firmly cut across what she knew would be Zak's much more embellished description of the man who lived in the apartment next door. 'I'm taking myself off to bed now; once you've cleaned up in here, I suggest the two of you do the same thing. You're going to have a busy morning ahead of you tomorrow, looking for somewhere else to stay,' she added with satisfaction.

Rik stood up slowly, over six feet tall, his manner and

speech reserved. 'It's good to see you too—Stazy,' he said pointedly.

Some of her anger faded as she saw the real hurt in his face. 'It is good to see you, Rik.' She crossed the room to give him a hug. 'It's just that two of you, in three days, is just too much!' She closed her eyes briefly and wearily.

'We only need Nik to turn up, and we'll be one big happy family again,' Zak announced insensitively.

Family. Yes, these two men, one so tall and blond, full of good humour, the other as tall but dark-haired, and much more introvert, were two of her older brothers. Nik was the third. And last, thank goodness. If he turned up, she would be the one to move out and just leave them to it!

Much as she loved her brothers, they just didn't seem to understand that they were part of the reason she had moved back to England in the first place. She didn't intend to have a repeat over here of what had been happening in her life during the last three years!

But if Zak and Rik had found her, then she knew that Nik wouldn't be far behind...

'Oops.' Zak grimaced as he saw Stazy's unhappy expression. 'Is Nik still the big bad ogre in your book?'

'What do you think?' she scorned, moving out of the curve of Rik's arm. 'As I said, I'm going to bed. I'll see you both in the morning—before you leave!'

When would they realise that she was all grown up now? Stazy thought to herself as she prepared for bed. Probably never, she acknowledged grudgingly. To them she would always be their little sister, someone they felt needed protecting. The only people she needed protecting from was them!

It hadn't been so bad during the years she was away

at boarding-school in England, but when she was eighteen, and had moved back to the States, their overprotectiveness had become a nightmare. Nik, as the oldest, had been the worst, usually ensuring that one or more of her brothers was with her wherever she went.

The problem was they were all so much older than her; Rik was the youngest at thirty-three, twelve years her senior, Zak was thirty-five, and Nik thirty-eight. In fact, Nik had always acted more like a Victorian father than her oldest brother. Was it any wonder she had rebelled? But Nik, being Nik, had simply tightened the reins on her. With disastrous results. He had simply gone too far in the end as far as Stazy was concerned, their struggle ending suddenly three months ago when she had walked out of the family home after telling Nik she never wanted to see him again!

She still didn't want to see him. He had messed up her life. Not all by himself, she accepted that, but he had been ultimately responsible for what had happened.

But he had to be behind Zak and Rik turning up here, she was sure. Nik was the one with all the contacts, and would be able to work out that Stazy Walker was her—

She turned sharply towards the door as, after the briefest of knocks, Rik strolled into her bedroom. Privacy was something else they never allowed her, either!

She looked across at her brother from where she was lying back against the pillows. 'Yes, Rik?' Her annoyance at his intrusion was barely masked.

Although, in truth, Rik was the one she had always been the closest to, he being the nearest to her in age. It was good to see him, she admitted secretly. Zak, too. Although she would never tell either of them that!

He held something up in his hand. 'Jordan said you forgot to take this with you when you left earlier—'

'Jordan?' she echoed sharply, sitting upright in bed, not realising that she looked very young without make-up, wearing an American football top as a nightgown. 'Jordan was here?' She cringed at the thought. She certainly hadn't heard the doorbell. Too busy grumbling to herself, probably, she conceded.

Rik nodded unconcernedly. 'He said you forgot to take the key to his apartment so you can get in tomorrow. I'll put it here, shall I?' He indicated the dressing-table beside him.

'Fine,' she accepted distractedly. 'Did—?' She swallowed hard. 'Did he say anything else?' Like, Who the hell are you? She groaned inwardly.

'Just goodnight,' her brother replied. 'He seemed an okay sort of guy.'

High praise, indeed! Although she doubted Jordan would have been too impressed by it, if he'd heard it. 'Okay enough for Nik to approve of?' she derided.

Rik grinned, and it was a grin worth waiting for, deepening the blue of his eyes, showing the laughter-lines beside his eyes and mouth, his usual reserve momentarily dispelled. 'I wouldn't go that far!'

'No!' she accepted heavily. If Nik had his way, she would be a nun. At a convent of *his* choice, of course!

'Jak—'

'The name is Stazy,' she corrected him hardly.

Her mother's choice of names for her four children: Nikolas—Nik, Zakary—Zak, Rikard—Rik, and for herself Jakeline—Jak had been a constant source of amusement to people for years. Stazy had dispensed with that at the same time she'd moved to England, preferring her middle name of Stazy, and her mother's maiden name of Walker. And her brothers—all of them!—despite their obvious reluctance, could damn well use it! As she had told them earlier, she was no longer a part of the act!

'I would rather not talk about Nik,' she told Rik flatly. 'Stazy—'

'Thanks for bringing me the key,' she went on, her gaze steadily determined.

With a grimace of acceptance, Rik left her bedroom, closing the door quietly behind him.

Stazy got slowly out of bed to look at the key he had put on her dressing-table. Jordan's key. What on earth must he be thinking, having found yet another man in her apartment?

Or perhaps Jordan wasn't thinking anything at all. Perhaps it was of no particular importance or interest to him how many men she had in her life!

CHAPTER FOUR

'ANOTHER one,' Jordan muttered to himself as he slammed the door to his apartment behind him.

Damn it, how many men did Stazy have in her life? Because, despite what she had said earlier, neither of the two he had met so far remotely resembled frogs!

Why should he care?

He didn't!

Oh, but he did, he realised. Stazy Walker was like a breath of fresh air on a hot summer's day, completely unaffected, her beauty unquestionable, her humour infectious; she had even managed to make him smile once or twice this evening!

Then wasn't it only natural that other men should gravitate towards her warmth and beauty?

Of course it was, he answered himself impatiently, but did they actually have to stay in her apartment? And two of them at the same time…! But she had acted as if she were shocked at some of the suggestions made to her by supposed clients!

Hell, he was the one who was shocked. She had seemed so young, innocent almost—

'Seemed' was the right word, he told himself, picking up a half-full bottle of whisky and a glass; it was going to be a long night, he decided. How could it be anything else with Stazy snugly ensconced next door with those two more-than-handsome men?

*　*　*

57

'Just say if I'm keeping you up, Jordan,' Jarrett drawled dryly.

Jordan scowled across the width of the desk at his oldest brother, the sunlight which was shining through the window behind Jarrett enough to make him give a pained wince. A night with half a bottle of whisky, empty by the time he fell asleep, was not conducive to concentration the next day, he had discovered; Jarrett was right in his assumption that Jordan hadn't been listening to a word he said! And they were meant to be discussing a contract they were going to put on the table this afternoon.

'I have a headache,' Jordan mumbled—he had a hangover that made him feel as if a drum was being banged—loudly—inside his head.

Jarrett leaned back in his chair. 'A raw egg and Worcester sauce,' he recommended.

If Jordan could have opened his eyes properly in this sunlight he would have glared, but, as it was, all he could do was deepen his scowl. 'I said I have a headache, Jarrett, not a hangover,' he corrected coldly.

Dark brows rose sceptically over golden eyes. 'Would the headache's name happen to be Stazy?'

Jordan was not in the mood for his brother's particular brand of sarcastic humour. 'No—its name wouldn't happen to be Stazy,' he rasped harshly. 'She doesn't even come into the equation!'

Jarrett watched him knowingly. 'And what equation would that be?' he asked slowly.

'Don't try and play word games with me, Jarrett,' Jordan bit back. 'Just because you and Jonathan have fallen into the marriage trap doesn't mean every other man has to be as stupid!'

His brother smiled. 'I'm not altogether sure you're

being complimentary to Abbie and Gaye. Neither am I sure why marriage came into the conversation…? Ah, yes, we were talking about Stazy,' he said softly, his expression once again mocking.

'*You* were talking about Stazy, *I* was complaining of a headache,' Jordan protested. 'And talking of headaches, what have you done with Stella?' He watched as Jarrett's expression turned from humour to icy disdain.

Not that Jordan particularly wanted to discuss Stella either, but by the same token it was preferable to talking about Stazy any more. He wasn't sure where she fitted at all!

Jarrett visibly forced himself to relax. 'Nice try, Jordan,' he responded with an acknowledging inclination of his head. 'But we'll get back to Stazy in a moment. Stella, in the meantime, has been put on hold.'

Jordan gave a snort of disbelief. 'How the hell do you put Stella on hold?'

Jarrett's mouth quirked. 'You tell her you need time to think over her request for money—at least, until your brother is safely away on his honeymoon!'

Jordan's eyes widened. 'And that actually worked?' He didn't for a moment believe his mother had actually listened to what *he* had to say on Saturday!

'Temporarily,' Jarrett confirmed harshly. 'She certainly knew how to pick her moment!'

She always had. He and Jonathan hadn't known until a long time afterwards about the money Jarrett had given their mother ten years ago, after the collapse of her second marriage, just to keep her out of the lives of his two younger brothers.

'Her request to see her grandson was, of course, flatly refused,' Jarrett added. 'I'm not letting her anywhere near my family,' he said bleakly.

Find the weak spot, and go for it… Yes, that sounded like Stella. Roll on husband number four, was Jordan's fervent wish. With any luck they then wouldn't see Stella again for a while!

Jarrett's expression softened. 'Now about Stazy—'

'Forget it, Jarrett,' Jordan cut in laughingly, standing up. 'She just happens to be my next-door neighbour—'

'The freckly redhead you first mentioned a few months ago?' Jarrett realised incredulously. 'Good God, Jordan, you've either been blind—or you've been keeping your relationship with her to yourself! Stazy is beautiful!'

And Jordan hadn't even seen her, really seen her, until Saturday evening. By that time *she* had seen *him*—though not in any favourable light, he remembered with an inward groan of self-reproach.

'Half the male population of America seems to be in agreement with you,' Jordan rejoined grimly. 'There have been two of them going in and out of her apartment, one for the last three days,' he admitted reluctantly at Jarrett's questioning look. Although he wasn't about to tell his brother that the two men were staying with Stazy!

Jarrett's shout of laughter did not make him feel any less of an idiot. Because that was exactly how he felt where Stazy was concerned. He couldn't work her out at all. She seemed so innocent, and yet the presence of the blond giant and the broody dark-haired man seemed to say otherwise…

'You *have* been blind.' Jarrett still chuckled—much to Jordan's annoyance.

'Don't you dare tell Abbie any of this,' Jordan warned. 'She'll tease me mercilessly—or invite Stazy to dinner.' Which was exactly what his sister-in-law had done in an effort to matchmake with Jonathan and Gaye. And look what had happened to them!

'I won't tell Abbie,' Jarrett assured him, 'as long as you tell me what you're going to do to rectify the situation.' He raised dark brows challengingly.

'What makes you think I'm—? Okay.' Jordan held up protesting hands as Jarrett reached for the telephone— to call Abbie, no doubt! 'I've hired myself an interior designer to decorate my apartment,' he admitted reluctantly, knowing exactly what Jarrett was capable of if he felt so inclined.

Jarrett looked at him blankly. 'And?'

Jordan shrugged. 'That's it.'

Jarrett grimaced, shaking his head. 'Is this in the hope that the noise from the decorators will so disturb Stazy, she'll come to investigate? I have to tell you, Jordan—' he gave another shake of his head '—that's probably the lamest plan I ever heard for getting a woman interested. Besides being expensive! Wouldn't a bouquet of flowers have been a little easier to arrange, besides being—?'

'Not if the interior designer is Stazy herself,' Jordan cut in before his brother could make any more derisory remarks. 'Now if you'll excuse me, I think an early lunch might revive me enough to get me through the afternoon!' The last thing he felt like doing was eating, but other than the raw egg and Worcester sauce Jarrett had recommended earlier—and it turned his stomach just to think of that!—food was probably his best bet.

He left the office to the sound of Jarrett's continued chuckles. Whether with him or at him, he wasn't sure...

Stazy had been in his apartment while he was out at work. He could smell her perfume as he came in the door. She had been, and then gone again, but her per-

fume remained, somehow as elusive as the woman herself. And somehow just knowing she had been in here,
and then left again, made his apartment seem suddenly
very empty...

Which was ridiculous. His apartment was empty, the
way it always was, which was what he had always liked
about it. He valued his privacy, the solitude he could
find in his apartment, away from his brothers, away from
work. Away from everyone!

And yet his apartment seemed even emptier for knowing Stazy's brief presence...

But it wasn't completely without her, he realised as
he went through to the kitchen. He could smell something cooking. Something very appetising. There was a
large piece of yellow paper stuck on his fridge door with
a magnet—a large yellow smiling face magnet, he noticed incongruously—that hadn't been there when he'd
left for work this morning.

'Your dinner is in the oven keeping warm,' he read,
'as a thank-you for giving me dinner last night. Wine is
open and ready to drink. Stazy.'

But he hadn't actually cooked their meal the evening
before; he'd merely picked the food up on his way home
from work. However, Stazy had obviously cooked something for him. Chilli with rice, he discovered after check-
ing in the oven. And she had left it for him to eat at his
leisure. The wine, a rather nice red, was, as she said,
open and ready for him to drink.

Which he did want to at that moment, pouring himself
a glass before slumping down on one of the pine chairs
at his kitchen table.

Stazy had cooked him dinner!

Part of him was quite touched by the gesture—and the
other part of him went into panic. What did it mean?

Was it as innocently neighbourly as it appeared—or
something else? She wasn't going to start doing his laun-
dry too, was she? Wafting about the place with a duster
in her hand? Several friends of his had been caught in
domestic traps like that, and—

He was being unfair to Stazy. Why should she bother
trying to trap him, when she already had two men in
residence? The food she had prepared was exactly what
it seemed; if anything, it was probably a debt Stazy felt
she had towards him for feeding her the evening before.

But that didn't make him feel any more cheerful either!

Jarrett was right; he had been blind for the last three
months. Stazy was beautiful. He had been behaving like
an idiot. Well, no more!

She looked younger than ever when she opened her
door to him a while later, Jordan having abandoned his
wineglass and paused only long enough in his own apartment to change out of his business suit into denims and
a navy blue shirt. Her hair was tied back at her nape
with a black ribbon, revealing those freckles he had mentioned to Jarrett months ago. A 'freckly redhead'—was
that really how he had described her? She looked very
casual in a loose black shirt worn over black leggings,
her feet bare. God, even her feet were pretty, Jordan
noticed.

'Hello,' she greeted. 'Don't tell me, you don't like
chilli! My mistake; I always assume everyone likes spicy
food as much as I do,' she said self-deprecatingly, moving back so he could step inside her apartment. 'As you
can see, I was just about to sit down to dinner myself.'
She gestured as he took in the dining-table set for one
person, a plate of steaming hot chilli and rice already on

the table, an identical bottle of wine to the one she had left in his apartment open on the table too.

Where were the two men? Jordan wondered. But only briefly. He and Stazy were eating exactly the same meal, drinking the same wine, but separately!

'What are you doing?' Stazy frowned as he picked up her plate of food and the bottle of wine.

He smiled at her. 'I love chilli.' He spoke for the first time since entering her apartment. 'But I would prefer it if the chef joined me while I ate! Come next door and we can eat together,' he invited as she gave him a quizzical glance.

She hesitated. 'Wouldn't you rather be alone?'

'No. Unless you would?' He looked at her questioningly. She seemed to have had rather a lot of company over the last three days; maybe she had been looking forward to a quiet evening to herself...?

She grinned, those freckles on her nose looking endearing. 'To be quite honest,' she confided as she followed him to his apartment, her feet still bare on the carpeted floors, 'I couldn't wait for Zak and Rik to leave, but once they had my place suddenly seemed very empty! Stupid, huh?' she said, helping him set the kitchen table for them both to eat.

Not really. His apartment had felt exactly the same way when he'd arrived home earlier. 'Zak and Rik?' he repeated casually.

Was it his imagination—because he was watching for her reaction so closely!—or did she suddenly avoid his gaze? Because her answer, when it came, really wasn't much help where the two men were concerned.

'Friends from home,' she dismissed lightly. 'They have moved into a hotel now.'

Well, that, at least, was a relief. Although he still

found their presence in her apartment at all somehow puzzling...

'I found some wonderful material for your sitting room today,' she told him. 'I'll show it to you after dinner, if you like.'

The decoration of his apartment was a safe subject, Jordan guessed ruefully, not fooled for a minute by Stazy's change of subject. But just watching her as she talked was fascinating in itself. She had such an animated face, her mouth wide and smiling, those beautiful deep blue eyes alight with enthusiasm. She certainly loved the work she did.

Would she look this way when in the arms of the man she loved?

What the hell—? Where had *that* come from? What did it matter to him how she would look with the man she loved? Was he completely—?

'Is the chilli too hot?' Stazy looked concerned by the sudden scowl on his face.

'Not at all.' He answered her abruptly, for the next few minutes concentrating on his food to the exclusion of all else. Including Stazy. His thoughts about her were becoming too wild for comfort. His comfort! In fact, if he attempted to stand up at this moment it could be very embarrassing for both of them!

He was responding to Stazy's beauty like a callow schoolboy! He had been out with dozens of women, most of them as beautiful—if not more so—as Stazy. And yet he had felt warmed this evening just at the sight of her again. His body ached with desire for her...!

This was not the time for this, he told himself. He was too angry at the moment, too consumed with resentment towards his two brothers, for what he believed was their desertion by falling in love and getting married, to be able to deal with any relationship himself with any degree of detachment. But detached was how he intended to remain!

'You have good taste in wine,' he told her as he took an appreciative sip. It was rich and fruity, a perfect complement for the chilli.

Stazy gave a smile. 'My brother made sure of that,' she admitted. 'He told me that a woman has to be good for something—if only for choosing the right wine to go with the meal!' she sighed.

She had a brother; Jordan filed that piece of information away in the part of his memory that was marked 'Stazy'. A chauvinistic brother, by the sound of it. Older than her too, Jordan would guess. And he knew only too well how frustrating it could be to have older brothers!

'Does your family live in America?' he prompted casually—she had a way of never really discussing herself, he had noticed, while at the same time giving the impression of being very open...

'You already know about my father. My mother is dead; she died three years ago,' she revealed tonelessly, her expression suddenly closed. 'That's one of the reasons this move to London seemed so natural,' she continued stiltedly. 'There was nothing left to hold me in the States.'

'Not even a man?' Jordan teased, finding it hard to believe there hadn't been a boyfriend in her life.

'Especially not a man!' she bit out.

Jordan was taken aback. 'Not even your brother?'

'Most especially not him.' Her voice hardened angrily. 'I would really rather not talk about him any more, if you don't mind.'

It wasn't a request, but a statement of fact. Stazy was

as angry with her brother as Jordan felt with his own. Something else they had in common...

'Let's clear this stuff away.' He stood up to move their empty plates. 'And then you can show me this wonderful material,' he said lightly.

Her mouth quirked. 'I'm still not altogether sure you're taking this—or me!—seriously, Jordan,' she chided as she cleared the table while he stacked the dishwasher.

'Believe me, Stazy,' he told her, 'I'm in no mood to take anything in any other way but seriously.'

She gave him a questioning look, but the set of his features must have warned her off pursuing the subject any further, in the same way her own expression had done a few minutes ago concerning her brother.

'I'll go get the swatch,' she announced in a business-like tone.

She was right: the material was a beautiful, thick brocade, and there were numerous shades to choose from; Jordan finally opted for a rich russet brown, for the curtains and to cover the suite he already had. The rest of the room he would leave for Stazy to blend in around these main features.

Jordan sat back, the two of them having settled themselves down on the carpet in the sitting room, the material samples scattered around them. 'I never realised this sort of thing could be fun.' He sounded surprised, because he was. The reason his apartment had kept the same decor since he moved in was that he simply couldn't face changing it. Stazy made sure it wasn't a chore...

She laughed huskily at his obvious surprise. 'Too many visions of men being dragged from store to store by a determined wife! I love all this.' She indicated the scattered swatches. 'And the transformation all the work can achieve.' She looked about them appreciatively. 'I can already see how marvellous this room is going to look,' she assured him, her face alight with pleasure. 'You're going to love it, Jordan!'

Jordan stared at her as a terrible realisation hit him forcibly in the face. *Stazy* would look marvellous in this room that was going to be decorated with golds and russet browns. He realised it had been thoughts of her that had steered him towards those colours...

He stood up quickly, brushing several threads of material from his denims. 'I'm sure you're right,' he said harshly. 'As long as I don't have to be too involved in it.' Or with her, he amended determinedly to himself.

'Of course not,' she assured him with a frown, hastily picking up the swatches of material before standing up. 'We'll do it one room at a time, so as not to create too much of a muddle for you.'

This whole thing was already a muddle as far as he was concerned! He wanted this woman, but he didn't want the complication of her. And somehow he knew Stazy would be a serious complication!

'Fine,' he acknowledged abruptly. 'Now, if you'll excuse me, I have some work of my own to catch up on.'

'Of course.' There was an embarrassed flush to her cheeks now. 'I'm sorry if I've taken up too much of your time.'

Now she was uncomfortable for intruding—and he was a heel for making her feel that way! And he didn't like knowing that at all. A complication? Yes, Stazy Walker was one, all right!

'You didn't,' he replied tersely. 'I just have some papers I have to look through before tomorrow. But dinner was great, thanks. And go ahead and order the material;

I'm sure it's going to look fine.' Even if he was reminded of Stazy, of her long, luxuriant red hair, every time he looked at it! Maybe having her come in and out of his apartment at will wasn't such a good idea, after all... 'Stazy, I—' He broke off as the telephone rang, frowning across at it darkly; the number of people who knew this private number were limited...

'I'll leave you to take your call,' Stazy told him hastily.

'No. Wait.' He held up a protesting hand; he couldn't let her depart like this again. He would end up downing another half a bottle of whisky, and on top of the wine he had already consumed that would not be a good idea! 'Yes?' he barked into the receiver after snatching it up impatiently.

'Is she any good?'

Jordan didn't need to ask who the caller was, instantly recognising Jarrett's voice. He also didn't need to ask who 'she' was!

He glanced across at Stazy as she waited awkwardly across the room. 'At what?' he returned hardly.

'Interior designing, of course,' Jarrett answered him with laughter in his voice. 'You can keep anything else she's good at to yourself!'

'I wouldn't know,' Jordan answered him dryly. 'But exactly why are you interested?' he prompted warily.

'I mentioned to Abbie—'

'So much for keeping your word which you gave me only this morning!' Jordan cut in impatiently. 'You told me you wouldn't tell Abbie anything!'

'That Stazy is an interior designer,' Jarrett continued unconcernedly. 'She's decided that Charlie's bedroom needs decorating, and—'

'That's very sudden, isn't it?' Jordan derided this urgent necessity for his step-niece to have her bedroom redecorated.

'You know women, Jordan—'

'I know Abbie, Jarrett,' he interrupted. 'She's an interfering busybody—'

'That happens to be my wife you're talking about, Jordan,' his brother protested in a steely voice. 'And you know she cares for you very much—'

'Could you ask her to care about me in some other way?' Jordan demanded. 'Preferably one that doesn't involve my personal life!'

'None of this changes the fact that Abbie has decided Charlie's bedroom needs decorating,' Jarrett told him briskly. 'Or that you know an interior designer we could use for the job. Abbie feels that perhaps Charlie has felt a little left out of things since Conor was born, and that giving her the treat of choosing new wallpaper and curtains for her room might make her feel better about it.'

Jarrett was well aware of how much Jordan loved Charlie, how he couldn't bear the thought that she might feel even a little less special than she always had been, to all of them...

'For God's sake, Jordan,' Jarrett went on. 'Abbie just wants to talk to the woman, that's all—'

'Oh, to hell with this,' Jordan exploded. 'Tell Abbie she can talk to her right now!' He held the receiver out to Stazy. 'It's for you,' he stated grimly.

Stazy gave him a startled look. 'Me? But I don't—'

'My sister-in-law would like a few words with you.' His mouth twisted derisively as Stazy reluctantly took the receiver from him.

Jordan deliberately chose not to listen to Stazy's part in the conversation with Abbie, going through to the kitchen to pour himself another glass of wine—and forget the consequences! Work could wait for another evening. Because if he had Abbie on his case he had much more of a problem than trying to keep his hands off Stazy!

CHAPTER FIVE

STAZY found Jordan in the kitchen once she had concluded her conversation with Abbie Hunter. 'That was very kind of you,' she said.

His scowl wasn't exactly welcoming. 'What was?' he replied without interest, taking a sip of wine from his glass.

'Recommending my work to your sister-in-law.' Stazy was determined not to leave until she had at least said thank you. Work commissions had been few and far between since she'd arrived in London, although she had always known it would only take one or two clients to get her business moving, that the rest would follow by word of mouth. As it had in this case.

Jordan looked sceptical. 'Is that what I did?'

According to Abbie Hunter—yes! But even if that wasn't exactly what had happened—and Jordan's attitude seemed to say it wasn't!—it ultimately wouldn't matter; her work would rise or fall on its own merits. And she had confidence enough to believe it would rise!

'Yep, that's me,' Jordan continued self-mockingly. 'Kindness is my middle name.' He stood up.

She couldn't say she was exactly comfortable with the way his mood had suddenly changed from how it was a short time ago—and men accused women of being changeable!

'I'll leave you to get on with your evening now,' she decided. It had been a good day so far: Zak and Rik had moved out to a hotel, things were moving ahead with the decoration of Jordan's sitting room, another job was already lined up; she would quit while she was still ahead!

Jordan sighed. 'I've lost interest,' he confessed. 'Have another glass of wine,' he invited heavily.

'Thanks, but I have some work to do,' she told him brightly; she wasn't about to let his own negative mood affect her positive one. After months, it seemed, of swimming against the tide, she was finally flowing with it. 'Don't worry about my dishes,' she assured him as she turned to leave. 'I'll pick them up some time tomorrow.' When he wasn't here!

It had been a mistake to have dinner with him this evening, she realised. They might be next-door neighbours, but it was probably best if they kept their relationship on a purely business footing. It could only complicate matters if they were to become too friendly with each—

Kissing her was not businesslike!

But that was exactly what Jordan was doing. Again!

Stazy stood unresistingly in his arms. Unresisting, but not responsive either. She didn't understand this man. One minute he was warm and friendly—at the moment, too friendly!—and the next he could be as cold as ice. It was very unnerving. And totally confusing.

He drew back to look down at her, frowning darkly as he sensed her lack of response. 'No?' he rasped.

She gave a pained grimace. 'I don't understand you, Jordan—'

'Heaven protect me from a woman who understands me!' he pronounced grimly as he released her, moving back to where his glass stood on the table, taking a huge swallow from it. 'I don't understand you either, Stazy, but it doesn't stop me finding you attractive!'

Lack of understanding didn't stop her finding him attractive either! In fact, nothing seemed to stop her doing that. He was handsome and self-assured, witty and attractive—when he chose to be. But it was the latter she found so disturbing—she never knew when he was going to choose to be any of those things!

'I don't think either of us is interested in a relationship, Jordan,' she told him. 'So let's just stick to business, huh?'

Those golden eyes narrowed, and then he nodded curtly. 'Business,' he echoed abruptly.

She felt a little disappointed that he didn't even attempt to change her mind. It wasn't very flattering that he'd accepted her decision so easily, and her ego had taken a battering lately. Oh, well, it was done now...

'Fine,' she accepted shortly, turning to leave.

'Er—Stazy?' Jordan called out softly, arching dark brows teasingly when she turned back to him warily. 'Does this mean you won't be cooking me dinner again?'

She grinned her relief at the incongruousness of the question. 'It means that it's your turn to cook next time!'

'Eggs have been known to beg for mercy when I take them out of the box!' he warned.

She laughed, as much with relief at the passing of the tension between them as at the humour of the remark. She quirked auburn brows. 'I'm sure you're more than capable of beating them into submission!'

'Ouch!' He gave a pained wince at her deliberate pun. 'Okay, I'll cook next time,' he agreed as he walked her to the door.

'Leave it for a few days,' Stazy advised. 'I should have got some ideas moving by then,' she explained.

She also felt it would be better if they didn't see each

other for a while; things were getting altogether too difficult between them! Besides, she wanted to finish the job he had given her, not be dismissed before she even started!

'Thanks for the meal, Stazy,' Jordan told her awkwardly. 'I—enjoyed it.'

She looked at him searchingly, wondering if he was taunting again. But she could only see sincerity in his face. It had just been a chilli, just a double portion of what she was preparing for herself. But how often did someone cook him a meal…? Oh, she didn't mean the restaurant kind, or a takeaway like the one he had provided last night, but a meal actually cooked at home and served to him. Not very often, she would guess…

'My pleasure,' she told him warmly, walking the short distance to her own apartment, looking down suddenly at her bare feet. 'Very businesslike.' She turned back to Jordan as he still watched her from his apartment doorway.

Jordan was chuckling softly as she unlocked her door and went inside her flat.

Why was it, she wondered as she moved around her sitting room switching on the lamps, that one minute Jordan could be so pleasant and friendly, and the next he was cold and mocking?

If she knew the answer to that, then she would know the man, and, as he had said himself, 'Heaven protect me from a woman who understands me!'

Well, heaven protect the woman who understood him!

'What *are* you doing?'

The outburst, completely unexpected, was enough to make Stazy wobble precariously on the chair she was standing on. The material she was holding slipped to the floor as she grabbed the back of the chair to regain her balance.

'Jordan, you startled me,' she protested without turning. 'I was just—' But the rest of her words remained lodged in her throat as she finally turned and saw that Jordan wasn't alone!

Standing at his side across the room was a small, feline-looking blonde, her figure pure perfection in a black dress, her face a sculpture of beauty, although the eyes, green and also cat-like, were piercing now as she looked speculatively at Stazy.

Stazy, for her part, was horrified at what the other woman could see! Her hair was secured back at her nape, her face was bare of make-up, and she was wearing a loose white shirt that had once belonged to one of her brothers and faded denims that had seen better days. Her feet were bare once again as well—they always were unless she was forced to wear shoes because she was going out somewhere!

Looking at the woman with Jordan, they appeared to be the ones who were going out!

'You were just…?' Jordan prompted before the silence could stretch too uncomfortably.

But Stazy was already ill at ease as she stepped down onto the carpeted floor, self-consciously pushed back the loose tendrils of her hair away from her face. 'I—was just experimenting with a pelmet.' She pointed awkwardly in the direction where she had half pinned the material around the frame. 'I was hoping to get it done before you got home, so that you could look at it, and sit and think about it for a couple of days while I finish off the curtains.' From being speechless when they first arrived, she now couldn't seem to stop babbling!

'How domesticated, Jordan.' The tiny blonde turned

to him flirtatiously. 'You didn't tell me you had a house-keeper.' The last was said slightly sceptically—as if she didn't believe for a moment that Stazy was his house-keeper.

Stazy had no doubt what this woman thought she was, and she looked straight at Jordan as she waited for his answer.

'You don't know everything about me, Elaine,' he returned evenly. 'Isn't that the reason we're having dinner together this evening, so that we can get to know each other a little better?'

His omission in explaining exactly who Stazy was, and what she was doing here, was glaringly obvious. To Stazy herself. And to the hard-eyed blonde who no longer looked in the least like a pussy-cat. But then, neither would Stazy in the circumstances.

'I—'

'I only came back to change.' Jordan smoothly cut in on Stazy's own intended explanation for her presence here. 'I shouldn't be too long. I'm sure you two ladies can entertain each other while I'm gone.'

If he was meaning to be funny, then neither Stazy nor the beautiful Elaine saw the joke!

Having recovered from her surprise at his early return, Stazy now felt more than a little annoyed that Jordan hadn't explained she was his interior designer; the only other role left open to her, in the circumstances, was far from acceptable to her! If Jordan thought she was going to take this lying down—or even standing up!—then he was in for a surprise himself!

'Help yourself to a drink, Elaine.' Jordan indicated an array of bottles on the side board. 'You too, Stazy, if you would like one,' he added, a devilish glint in his eyes as he left the room to go and change out of his business suit.

That devilishness Jordan had confessed to at the wedding reception…!

He was enjoying himself, damn him—at her expense! Well, two could play at that game…

'Shall we?' She held up a bottle of dry sherry for Elaine's approval.

'Why not?' The other woman sat down in one of the armchairs; judging by her expression, she was no happier than Stazy at this unorthodox situation.

Stazy poured two glasses of sherry, handing one to Elaine before sitting down in the armchair opposite, her bare feet curled up beneath her, no longer visible.

No doubt if she hadn't been here the other couple would have indulged in a little more than Elaine having a glass of sherry and Jordan changing his clothes; after all, it was only a little after seven o'clock, unfashionably early to be going out for a meal. But that was still no excuse for the way Jordan had just dumped Stazy in the middle of this awkward situation!

'Have you known Jordan long?' she queried politely, sipping her sherry, the liquid instantly warming her stomach—reminding her of the fact that she had forgotten to eat today. Better not drink too much…

'No,' Elaine answered flatly, obviously disgruntled. 'How long have you and Jordan—? Do you actually *live* here?' she snapped sharply.

A lot depended on her next answer, Stazy knew that. But, really, Jordan had only himself to blame!

'Yes,' she answered evenly. The same building constituted 'here'—didn't it?

Elaine drew in a harsh breath, taking what looked like a much needed swallow of the sherry. 'I had no idea,' she finally said. 'The last time I was in London was four months ago, and Jordan didn't mention—'

'Oh, I only moved in three months ago,' Stazy answered her quickly.

So Jordan and this woman really didn't know each other very well yet... And, from the angry glitter in those cat-like green eyes, Stazy had a feeling there was a stormy evening ahead for Jordan. Maybe next time he would think twice before attempting to play games. This was rather like responding to a small child's dare—and, at thirty-five, Jordan ought to know better!

'Three months...!' Elaine put down her empty sherry glass. 'But he's calmly brought me home, another woman whom he intends taking out to dinner. What sort of man is he?' she asked incredulously.

'Oh, Jordan can be very kind,' Stazy told her earnestly, looking, she knew, very young and innocent. 'He's been very good to me since I moved here from America.'

'Kind? Good?' Elaine echoed in a scandalised voice, standing up to refill her own glass. 'My dear girl—exactly how old are you?' Her eyes narrowed.

'Twenty-one,' Stazy supplied promptly.

'A mere child to a man of Jordan's years and experience,' Elaine dismissed angrily, her own age somewhere in the mid-thirties. 'It isn't kind of Jordan to bring home another woman!' she declared.

Stazy was casual. 'You aren't the first, and I doubt you'll be the last.' Which was also true; Jordan might be turned off by marriage, but he certainly wasn't turned off by women in general. Elaine was proof of that. As was the woman Stella who had turned up at his brother's wedding.

'But this is terrible.' Elaine was obviously shocked by

this whole situation. 'Why on earth do you put up with it? Why do you stay with someone who treats you like this?' She sounded furious at the humiliation Jordan was apparently doling out to his live-in lover.

'I don't have anywhere else to go,' Stazy told her truthfully.

Elaine shook her head. 'Incredible! I— You aren't pregnant, are you?' She looked at Stazy's loose white shirt.

Could she be? Could she go that far? Probably not, Stazy decided disappointedly. But, she also decided, Jordan was going to be angry enough already, without her embellishing things any more than she already had.

'Heavens, no.' Stazy gave a bright laugh. 'Jordan would never allow that.'

'No.' Elaine's mouth tightened. 'I don't suppose he would.' She took another sip of the sherry. 'Do you mind if, as an older woman, I give you some advice, Stazy?'

'Not at all,' she replied. She had absolutely nothing against this woman; it was Jordan she was annoyed with. While Elaine wasn't exactly the sort of person she would choose as a good friend—Elaine looked far too old and calculating for that!—Stazy had nothing against hearing what she had to say.

'Dump him,' Elaine told her vehemently. 'You're young and attractive, and you shouldn't allow any man to treat you in this way!'

Stazy's eyes were deliberately wide and innocent. 'But Jordan is so good-looking—'

'And I'm sure he's good in bed, too.' The other woman scorned her apparent naivety. 'Find a man that isn't, assure him he is—and then marry him! Believe me, I've been married twice to men like that, and they're the ones that stay faithful!'

This woman's first statement told Stazy all too clearly that Elaine was only guessing at Jordan's prowess in bed, that she had no evidence of it herself—yet. Though she was probably right, of course...

'But if you've been married twice...?' Elaine's ring-less hand said she was no longer married at all...

'Oh, they were boring, darling,' Elaine dismissed with a tinkling laugh. 'But if you choose a rich one it can make things more bearable. The divorce settlement more than makes up for a few wasted years.' She put down her empty sherry glass for the second time, turning to pick up her evening bag. 'Tell Jordan thanks—but no, thanks!' She walked purposefully towards the door.

Stazy stood up hurriedly. Elaine was leaving! She had meant to make things difficult for Jordan, not actually have his date walk out on him!

'Elaine!' she called out desperately, catching up with her at the door. 'Wouldn't you rather wait and talk to Jordan rather than just—?'

'Certainly not!' Elaine gave a contemptuous snort, putting a conciliatory hand on Stazy's arm. 'And do think about what I said, darling. No man is worth what Jordan is putting you through—no matter how good he is in bed!'

She left behind her the heady aroma of her perfume...but Stazy had a feeling that wasn't going to be enough for Jordan! He was going to be absolutely furious when he found Elaine had walked out on him. Perhaps she should just leave quietly herself, before he came back and—

'Where's Elaine?'

Too late! Stazy swallowed hard, turning slowly to face Jordan. He looked wonderful, she noticed incongruously, the black evening suit and showy white shirt, black bowtie telling her that he had intended taking Elaine to an up-market restaurant. But now there was no Elaine to take...

Stazy grimaced. 'Er—she had to leave,' she told him in a rush, not quite able to meet his gaze. 'She said to say thank you, but she—she had to go.' Taking with her the firm belief that Stazy was Jordan's lover.

When she chanced a glance at Jordan beneath thick dark lashes, it was to find him watching her with intent. She had never seen Jordan angry, and she didn't particulary want to now, either!

'I'll be on my way too now,' Stazy told him politely. 'I'll finish off in here tomorrow.' She gave a dismissive wave of her hand towards the half pelmet she had managed to hang before he and Elaine had arrived.

'What did you say to Elaine to make her leave, Stazy?'

She had almost reached the door when she heard his softly spoken question behind her. Had almost made good her escape...

'Me?' She turned back to him with an innocently surprised expression.

'Yes—you,' Jordan confirmed, strolling further into the room. 'I've been trying to get rid of the damned woman all day—with no success. But I leave her alone with you for ten minutes and—hey presto—she's gone!'

She stared at him with wide blue eyes. 'You've—been—trying—to—get—rid—of—her...?' she repeated.

'I certainly have,' he grinned, pouring himself a glass of whisky. 'She's a business associate. She comes up to town every—'

'Four months,' Stazy guessed swiftly, her breathing shallow, her temper starting to blaze inwardly as she began to realise she might just have been used.

'Every four months,' Jordan echoed mockingly. 'On the last two occasions I've managed to avoid her more than obvious suggestions of dinner—and whatever!—but this time she wasn't taking no for an answer.' He shook his head sadly. 'Other than being downright rude to her—'

'I wouldn't have thought you would have any trouble with that,' Stazy snapped, her temper rising.

'Ordinarily, no,' he conceded. 'But business is business.'

'And you didn't want to upset a business associate!' Stazy finished, blazing.

'I don't think Jarrett would have been too happy if I had.'

'I've met Jarrett,' Stazy bit out impatiently, 'and I very much doubt he would expect you to go to bed with a woman just to keep her sweet!'

Jordan raise dark brows. 'Who said anything about going to bed with her?' he drawled.

'She did! I did!' Stazy came back furiously. 'At least, she assumed the two of us go to bed together,' she amended bluntly.

Jordan looked perfectly relaxed, not in the least annoyed or upset at the way things had turned out. 'And exactly what made her decide to leave?' he asked curiously.

He was just relieved the situation had been sorted out for him, whereas Stazy felt as if she had been set up. Oh, Jordan couldn't possibly have known she would be in his apartment when he arrived home with Elaine in tow, but certainly hadn't lost any time in using the situation to his advantage!

'You did—by not correcting the impression Elaine got when you first arrived!' Stazy glared at him. 'I just went on to tell her that you keep me here barefoot—not pregnant!—as your sexual slave. That you're good in bed, so I'm quite happy with the situation— This is not funny, Jordan,' she burst out exasperatedly as he could contain his humour no longer, giving in to a shout of laughter.

'I think it's very funny,' he choked when he was finally able to talk at all. 'My sex slave, hmm?' He broke into deep chuckles of laughter once again.

Stazy watched him, fascinated in spite of herself. It was the first time she had seen him laugh properly—and it was worth waiting for. Those laughter-lines beside his nose and mouth were put to full use, his eyes glowed deeply golden and all of the harshness had gone from his face, making him appear younger.

He sobered slowly, taking several steps towards her. 'So I'm good in bed, am I?' he murmured speculatively.

Stazy took a step backwards, not liking the way he was advancing on her with that determined glint in his eyes. 'Only theoretically,' she said hurriedly.

He had reached her side in two long determined strides, his arms moving easily about the slenderness of her waist. 'How about we test out the theory?' he suggested throatily.

She swallowed hard, her heart pounding in her chest at his close proximity. She licked her suddenly dry lips. 'I'm afraid I wouldn't have anything to test it against,' she told him huskily.

Jordan gave her a searching glance, frowning as she shyly met his gaze. 'You're a virgin,' he realised flatly.

Now it was Stazy's turn to frown. 'You don't have to make it sound like an insult!' She pulled away from him, finding no resistance to the move; in fact, Jordan looked slightly dazed. No doubt he preferred his women experienced, like the beautiful Elaine. Well, *she* wasn't—and she wasn't ashamed of the fact, either! Jordan had pulled away from her as if she had something contagious. Well, he needn't worry; it was nothing he could possibly catch!

'I wasn't being insulting, Stazy—'

'Oh, yes, you were—but it really doesn't matter,' she responded firmly. 'You're obviously ready to go out, and I'm sure you have a table booked somewhere nice—and I think dinner is the least you owe me for this little episode!' she told him determinedly. 'Give me ten minutes to change and I'll be ready to go out and eat with you.' She didn't wait for his answer, letting herself out of his apartment and striding down the corridor to her own flat.

She was shaking quite badly by the time she got inside and closed the door behind her, leaning heavily back against it. She had felt such a fool, after that encounter with Elaine and the conversation with Jordan that had followed it. But her brother Nik had taught her the best form of defence was to attack. Well, she had attacked—and now she was stuck with spending the evening with Jordan.

But had she attacked—or had she lost the battle before it had even begun...?

CHAPTER SIX

DINNER with Elaine? Or Stazy? There was no question which he would prefer! Especially with Stazy looking the way she did when she returned to his apartment after her specified ten minutes. It had been ten minutes well spent!

The short red dress she had changed into should have clashed with the deep copper colour of her hair, but somehow it only made her tresses look more lustrously red as they cascaded riotously down her spine. Her make-up was light, her lip-gloss the same red as her dress, her legs long and shapely beneath its short style. And she had put shoes on for the occasion too, also red. She looked like a rare, exotic butterfly, a splash of colour in the quiet, exclusive elegance of the restaurant he had booked a table at earlier today, albeit for Elaine and himself.

The last thing Stazy looked, as Jordan watched her over the rim of his wineglass, was a virgin...

He had been shaken earlier by that admission; he would be lying if he said otherwise—and Stazy had obviously not been pleased by his reaction.

But it was, he felt, in the circumstances, a normal one. For one thing, Stazy was so damned beautiful, he couldn't be the only man who had trouble keeping his hands off her! And, for another, there was Zak and Rik... He hadn't imagined the existence of those two men—first Zak, and then Rik—both staying with her at her apartment!

He still found it difficult to believe in her innocence. And that, no doubt, if she knew, would make her angry all over again.

It wasn't something he particularly wanted to rouse at this moment, but Stazy's temper was something worth seeing; her whole face became animated, those blue eyes flashed. She really was the most intriguing young lady he had met in a long time—if ever! Beautiful, fascinating, talented, not to mention innocent—Stazy Walker was a dangerous young lady!

'What have you decided to eat?' he prompted brusquely, determinedly cutting off his wayward train of thought.

She looked across at him with one teasingly raised brow. 'Are you still mad at me for making you bring me out to dinner?'

Mad didn't exactly describe his emotions at the moment, and there was no way he could stand up from the table even if he wanted to: his body would betray exactly what he was feeling!

'I never do anything I don't want to do, Stazy,' he stated.

'Really? That wasn't the impression I had earlier this evening!'

His mouth tightened. 'As far as I was concerned, that was a business dinner—no matter what Elaine may have thought to the contrary!'

Stazy grinned. 'Well, just think of this as a business dinner too: taking your interior designer out for doing a good job!'

'All you seem to have done so far is pin up half a pelmet,' he commented.

Her smile widened. 'In that case, it can only get better, can't it? And to answer your question, I've decided to eat the gravadlax followed by the chicken. Vegetables with the latter,' she added with relish as she closed her menu decisively.

'You'll get fat,' Jordan murmured teasingly, sure that Stazy had never had a problem with her weight. She was like a finely honed racehorse, sleek and beautiful, glowing with health and vitality.

'And ugly,' she sighed. 'And then I'll never lose my virginity,' she added self-derisively.

'Stazy,' Jordan sobered, 'contrary to what you may have thought earlier, your virginity is a pleasant surprise, not a liability.' In fact, he didn't think—not since his teens anyway, and he wasn't too sure about then, either!—that he had ever been out with a virgin.

'Sometimes it seems like a bit of unwanted luggage I have to carry around.' She grimaced with feeling.

That was another thing about this young woman which was so unusual—she openly discussed things most other people would shy away from. But, at the same time, she was still so much of a mystery to him. Where had she come from? Why? Her explanation that her mother was dead, so there was nothing to keep her in the States any more, didn't make a whole lot of sense when she also admitted her mother had died three years ago. What had Stazy been doing during those three years? Where was the brother she had mentioned, and why had he let such an innocent take off alone for a different country? If *he* were her brother— But he wasn't—thank goodness! Because his feelings towards Stazy were far from brotherly!

'That depends on the man you eventually marry,' Jordan told her gently—hating that unknown man already! 'The ideal of The Virgin Bride is so unusual nowadays that—'

'Jordan! How lovely to see you again!'

Before he could respond to the greeting he was enveloped in a heady cloud of perfume as a woman bent down to kiss him warmly on the cheek—that perfume, exclusive as the woman herself, told him exactly who it was doing the kissing.

'Marilyn!' He stood up to hug her. 'All alone?' he asked flirtatiously as he could see she was unaccompanied.

'Of course not.' This latest vision of beauty smiled at him in a playful rebuke. 'Benjamin will be joining me shortly; he was delayed at the clinic.'

'In that case, I insist you join the two of us until he arrives.' Jordan held out his own chair for Marilyn to sit down, signalling to the waiter to bring a third chair to the table.

Marilyn hesitated, looking at Stazy as she smiled warmly. 'I'm sure you would much rather have this young man all to yourself, wouldn't you, my dear?' She spoke with her usual husky warmth.

Jordan could see the stunned recognition on Stazy's face that Marilyn's appearance usually engendered in people. Or else she was just surprised to hear him addressed as 'young man'; at fourteen years her senior, Stazy would hardly think of him as such!

'Not in the least,' Stazy replied. 'I— You— How wonderful to meet you, Miss Palmer,' she said with genuine admiration. 'Jordan, you didn't tell me you were acquainted with famous actresses,' she chided lightly, obviously over her first surprise now, starting to relax again.

'Just the one,' he responded wryly. Marilyn had been an internationally acclaimed actress for over forty years now. 'And you didn't ask!'

'He's such a tease,' Marilyn laughed. They were all sitting down now, a third chair having been supplied with quiet efficiency; a third glass of the white wine was also being poured.

'Not only do I know Marilyn Palmer,' Jordan told Stazy proudly, 'I'm related to her! In some way.' He gave Marilyn an apologetic smile for not knowing quite in what way they could be described as being related.

Marilyn's blue eyes widened, a deep blue that had held film and theatregoers entranced for years. 'Why, I suppose we are. In some way!' Once more she laughed her delight at the idea. 'My daughter Gaye is married to Jordan's brother Jonathan,' Marilyn explained to the puzzled Stazy.

'I was at the wedding,' Stazy said slowly.

'Were you?' Marilyn frowned. 'I'm so sorry, I didn't get to meet you.' She shook her finger reprovingly at Jordan. 'Jordan, you are a naughty boy—and you still haven't introduced the two of us!'

'Stazy Walker, Marilyn Palmer,' he obediently announced.

Marilyn had this effect on most men, he had discovered. Aged in her mid-sixties, she certainly didn't look it, her beauty and voluptuous figure still making her an extremely attractive woman. As their good friend Ben Travis had discovered several months ago after being introduced to her, immediately becoming smitten. The two had quickly become inseparable, hence Jordan's initial teasing of Marilyn; if Marilyn were here, then it followed that Ben couldn't be too far away!

'How do you like living in England, Stazy?' Marilyn enquired interestedly, a woman of genuine warmth who had no trouble putting other people at their ease.

Stazy gave a rueful smile. 'It's become a little—hectic since meeting Jordan!'

He looked across at her, wondering exactly what she meant by 'hectic'! She seemed to have created havoc in his own life the last few days, but he couldn't see he'd had the same effect on hers!

'They're all such wonderful young men,' Marilyn said confidingly. 'I couldn't have wished for a better husband for Gaye than Jonathan. And he's a wonderful son-in-law, too. He's such a dear boy, always so caring and considerate.'

That didn't exactly sound like the Jonathan Jordan knew and loved, although there was no doubting his brother's deep love for Gaye, or his true affection for Marilyn.

'Add arrogant and domineering to that—and I might start to recognise him!' Jordan said sardonically, knowing Marilyn wouldn't have a word said against the newest member of her family.

'A little arrogance in a man is perfectly acceptable, even attractive,' Marilyn predictably defended. 'Don't you agree, Stazy?'

Jordan gave Stazy a sideways glance, knowing by the glow in her eyes, that mischievous quirk to her mouth that she was enjoying this conversation. So, strangely enough, was he...

'As long as it is only a little,' Stazy finally answered, giving Jordan, he was sure, a knowing look.

Arrogant? Was he? He had always thought Jarrett was the most arrogant in the family, with Jonathan running a very close second. But Stazy seemed to think he had his own fair share of arrogance too... Not that it seemed to bother her too much, if he did!

'Jonathan rang me yesterday,' Marilyn continued

gaily. 'He and Gaye are having the most marvellous time in Hawaii!'

'I'm sure they are,' Jordan acknowledged dryly. 'Was Gaye too tired to come to the telephone or did you speak to her as well?'

'You're being naughty again, Jordan.' Marilyn tapped him lightly on the hand. 'A mother doesn't discuss those sorts of things with her only daughter! But of course I spoke to Gaye as well. She sounds so happy.' She smiled approvingly.

Jordan turned to find Stazy looking at him, rather strangely, he felt, frowning his puzzlement. Or maybe it was that she found the subject of Jonathan and Gaye's happiness a little too personal too...? That could be it. Especially after their own conversation earlier!

'I...'

'Excuse me, Miss Palmer.' The waiter quietly interrupted their conversation. 'There's a telephone call for you.'

'Probably Benjamin.' Marilyn wrinkled her nose in affectionate exasperation. 'Saying he'll be even later still, or that he isn't going to get here at all!' She stood up. 'He's a wonderful man, so dedicated to his work,' she excused without rancour.

'Please join the two of us if Ben can't make it,' Jordan invited her. 'Tell him he can join us for coffee later...and I might even let him pay the bill!'

'I'll tell him.' Marilyn made her way out to the reception area, closely followed by several admiring glances as she did so.

'You didn't mind my inviting Marilyn to join us, did you?' Jordan turned to Stazy once they were alone.

'Not at all,' she replied instantly. 'She's wonderful, isn't she?'

Jordan relaxed slightly at her reply. He had made the invitation to Marilyn without even thinking about it, but in retrospect he probably should have asked Stazy first.

This was definitely a first for him—he couldn't ever remember feeling he should have okayed his actions with anyone before now! But Stazy was his date—well, she was now!—and—

Stop giving yourself excuses, he inwardly remonstrated with himself. The truth of the matter was, the conversation, before Marilyn's interruption, had been getting altogether too heavy for comfort. His comfort! Marilyn's presence had lifted the whole evening.

No doubt one day some man would be thrilled by Stazy's innocence on their wedding night—but it wouldn't be him!

'We all think so.' Jordan nodded in answer to Stazy's comment.

'All?' She raised auburn brows.

'The whole family.' He nodded again. 'You see—'

'The bill is on Benjamin!' Marilyn announced as she rejoined them. 'I knew it was a mistake to agree to meet him at a restaurant!' she sighed as she sat down again. 'The dear man works far too hard, though, of course, he's brilliant at what he does,' she continued with pride, obviously not in the least put out by Ben's delay.

'Ben is a doctor,' Jordan explained to Stazy economically; Ben was much more than that, but his work was as private as the man was himself.

'Now, my dears.' Marilyn smiled at them both with that warmth that was so much a part of her natural charisma. 'Are you sure the two of you wouldn't rather spend the evening alone? It really is very kind of you to ask me to join you, but—'

'It wasn't in the least kind.' Stazy was the one to

answer. 'I would be absolutely fascinated to hear some anecdotes about your career. And what you're working on now. Wouldn't we, Jordan?'

'We certainly would,' he agreed; he was more than happy to make this into a threesome, and if Ben did manage to join them later so much the better.

Although, in truth, Jordan didn't join in the conversation too much as they ate their meal, leaving it to the two ladies; Marilyn's constant trips to America earlier in her career meant that she had Stazy had several mutually interesting subjects they could talk about.

Stazy was perfectly happy in Marilyn's company, the two of them chatting away like old friends, and Jordan found he was quite content to just sit watching them as they talked. Stazy's face was once again animated, her whole face alight with pleasure when she laughed. From a fairly disastrous beginning, it was, Jordan decided, turning out to be a very successful evening...

'That was absolutely marvellous,' Marilyn said with satisfaction when they had finished eating. 'I— Just in time!' she cried after glancing over at the entrance of the restaurant. 'Benjamin has managed to join us for coffee, after all.' Her face glowed with pleasure as she watched his progress across to their table.

They made a striking couple, Jordan acknowledged as Marilyn stood up to receive Ben's kiss of greeting. Ben was so tall and elegant, his hair snowy white, and Marilyn was tiny and voluptuously beautiful at his side. It was wonderful that these two such special people had found happiness together in their sixties—

Whatever was he doing sitting here grinning like an idiot at the thought of two people—no matter what their ages!—falling in love? The next thing he knew, he would find himself smiling at babies in prams! None of it was for him. His brothers might have fallen into that trap, but he certainly wasn't going to! He liked his freedom, doing what he wanted, when he wanted—

The fact that he was actually justifying this, even to himself, worried him more than a bit...

'Will you excuse me for a moment?' Stazy interrupted his jumbled thoughts, her hand on his arm as she stood up. 'I don't feel too well,' she added hastily before hurrying from the table.

Jordan stood up too, making his own excuses to the other couple before chasing after Stazy. She looked terrible by the time he caught up with her, her face deathly white, those freckles on her nose livid against the paleness of her skin.

'What is it, Stazy?' He expressed his concern at the way she looked, grasping her upper arms as she would have continued walking away. 'Do you feel sick: What is it?' He looked at her searchingly; her eyes were huge and deeply shadowed; she was a stark contrast to the animated woman she had been for most of this evening!

Stazy glanced back fleetingly at the older couple now seated at the table. 'Perhaps it was something I ate,' she excused quickly. 'Let me go, Jordan.' She pulled at his firm grip on her arms. 'I—I don't want to be ill in front of your friends.'

His friends— And yet until a few moments ago he had been completely superfluous as the two women chatted away together as if they had known each other for years...

'Would you like me to ask Marilyn to come and—?'

'No!' Stazy cut in sharply. 'No, thank you, Jordan,' she continued more calmly. 'That won't be necessary. I'll only be a few minutes.'

He released her reluctantly. 'If you're sure...?' He

really didn't like the idea of her being alone when she looked this ill.

'Positive.' Stazy squeezed his arm reassuringly before disappearing into the powder room.

Only Jordan didn't feel in the least reassured...

CHAPTER SEVEN

STAZY couldn't stop shaking once she reached the powder room, dropping down onto one of the stools in front of an array of mirrors, although her own reflection held absolutely no interest for her; her thoughts were all inwards.

That man.

It was the same man whom she'd spotted at the wedding. The man she had seen across the room that evening as she'd danced with Jordan. The man whose presence there had made her flee so abruptly then...!

Now she had learnt his name was Ben...!

But, as she had told herself after the wedding reception, once she had calmed down, it was ridiculous to believe it was *him*. There must be hundreds of men his age called Ben, dozens of them doctors too. It couldn't be the same Ben. It just couldn't be. Life wasn't as neat as that. It couldn't be that cruel!

Stazy took a deep breath, knowing the minutes were quickly passing while she reasoned all this out in her head. But she couldn't stay hidden in here for ever. She would have to go back to the table and face them very soon.

But what if he was the man she knew? What would she do then?

Nothing, came the flat answer. He didn't know her. And her name was different—she gave thanks at that moment to whatever instinct had made her change it when she'd moved to England!

But it wouldn't be the same man, she told herself firmly. It *couldn't* be!

'Just keep telling yourself that, Stazy,' she muttered to herself as she checked her appearance, adding blusher to give colour to the paleness of her cheeks, refreshing her red lip-gloss, pulling a brush through her hair to give it, at least, the vitality she lacked herself at the moment.

She had received a shock, that was all. But it was all in her imagination. Although Stazy still wished Marilyn's 'brilliant' Ben was any other man than the man she'd spotted at the wedding reception last weekend...

Her three companions were seated around the table as Stazy made her way back across the restaurant, her progress slow—because she was still reluctant to come face to face with Ben. Even if he didn't turn to be who she thought he was, the man had still given her a tremendous shock!

Jordan and Ben stood up when she arrived at the table, Jordan looking at her concernedly, Ben's gaze merely curious. No doubt the latter *was* curious, because he was interested in Jordan's female companion in the same way all the Hunter family had been!

'All right now?' Jordan whispered close to her ear as he pulled back her chair for her to sit down.

'Fine.' She gave him a bright smile—probably over-bright, judging by the way his eyes narrowed on her sharply. 'Sorry about that.' She turned back to the older couple, still not quite able to look Ben in the face, her gaze passing over him unseeingly.

'Ben, this is Stazy Walker.' Jordan introduced her as he resumed his own seat. 'Stazy, Benjamin Travis.'

It *was* him!

She shook Ben's hand automatically, her own limp as

she fought desperately to keep control, suddenly feeling as if the world had gone mad around her. What had been the chances—?

None, she had assured herself when she'd left America, breaking away from her brothers, Nik in particular, to make a life for herself in London. For the last three months her life, although she had been a little short of work, had gone quite smoothly. But now this!

Benjamin Travis wasn't just a doctor, as Jordan had described him earlier, but a psychiatrist. Although at times she felt as if her brothers might drive her insane, they hadn't ever been enough for her to imagine her path would actually cross Ben Travis's. It had never occurred to her that they might meet on a social level!

'Stazy?' Jordan was still looking at her as if he expected her to faint at any moment.

Which she wouldn't do; she was made of much sterner stuff than that. She had been thrown a few minutes ago, that was all, but none of what she knew about Ben Travis altered the fact that he was obviously a close friend of Jordan's, or that the four of them were about to have coffee together.

'It's a shame you missed dinner, Ben.' She spoke in a friendly tone, still not quite able to look into that still handsome face. 'But it's lovely you were able to join us for coffee, after all.'

The older man put his hand over Marilyn's. 'She would never have forgiven me if I hadn't!' he teased, looking fondly at the older woman.

'I doubt any man would stand up Marilyn Palmer,' Jordan put in sincerely. 'I should watch it, Ben, or someone more attentive might try to step into your shoes!' he warned.

Stazy was glad of the few minutes' respite this bantering conversation between the two men was giving her. All she had to do was drink her coffee, and then she and Jordan could leave. She could do that—couldn't she? This situation was so unreal that she thought perhaps she could!

'Stazy is an interior designer, darling,' Marilyn told Ben.

'Really?' Ben looked at Stazy interestedly; he was a man with an air of distinction. 'Marilyn and I have bought a house together, but she—understandably—refuses to name our wedding day until we've finished decorating the new house. Perhaps you could—'

'I'm sure Marilyn is perfectly capable of choosing all that sort of thing herself,' Stazy responded. Marilyn was going to marry this man! But she was so nice, and he was nothing more than a—

'Actually, Stazy, I would welcome your input,' the older woman assured her warmly. 'How wonderful of you to think of it, darling.' She gave Ben a dazzling smile. 'You see, it's so long since I took on a big project like refurbishing a whole house,' she confided in Stazy. 'But Benjamin and I thought it was important we have a completely fresh start, with no—well, no other memories to intrude,' she explained.

How ironic! No memories, huh? When Stazy herself could so easily become Ben Travis's worst memory!

But she could understand the fresh start that Marilyn wanted to make; the other woman had been married to the actor Terence Royal for over forty years before his untimely death a couple of years ago.

'I would be glad to give you any help you might need,' Stazy assured Marilyn—hoping this was just social politeness and that the older couple would forget all about it as soon as the evening ended! 'Although I'm sure Jordan regrets ever telling his family and friends what I do for a living,' she added dryly, shooting him a glance.

She was absolutely convinced that Jordan's suggestion concerning the decorating of his own apartment had been made impulsively; he could certainly never have imagined that it would lead to half his family trying to employ her too!

'Not at all,' he returned smoothly. 'When is it you're going to see Abbie and Jarrett?' he prompted casually.

Too casually, was Stazy's guess. He obviously envisaged her becoming involved with his family and friends in this way. Well, he really needn't worry where Ben Travis and Marilyn were concerned, because although she had made the offer it had been exactly that; she would make sure, if they contacted her after this evening, that she was far too busy to help them. She liked Marilyn, but involvement with Ben Travis, of any kind, was the last thing she wanted!

'I'm going to see Abbie next Monday.' She deliberately emphasised the fact that it was only Jordan's sister-in-law she was meeting; contrary to what he might think, this was business for her, and as far as that was concerned she was a complete professional. On Monday Abbie Hunter would be her customer, not Jordan's sister-in-law, even though she was one and the same person. Abbie herself might have other ideas on that subject, but Stazy was not about to discuss Jordan, or her own relationship with him, at any time!

'Morning or afternoon?' Jordan questioned sharply.

So that he could make sure he was nowhere near at the time?

Okay, so dinner with her this evening had been rather foisted on him, as recompense for leaving her to the hard-bitten mercy of the beautiful Elaine, but he hadn't seemed to mind his change of dining companion too much at the time. In fact, he had suggested testing out the theory of his being good in bed! Until she had admitted her inexperience to him. Maybe that was what troubled him…

'Afternoon,' she supplied slowly, a troubled expression marring her brow.

He nodded abruptly. 'In that case, I can drive you there. I don't have any appointments on Monday afternoon, and—'

'You really don't have to go to that trouble, Jordan.' She gasped her surprise at the offer. He had seemed most displeased the other day when Abbie had asked to speak to her, but now he was offering to drive her to his brother's home! So that he knew what the two women talked about…?

'The house isn't that easy to find,' Jordan concluded as if she hadn't spoken.

She gave a determined shake of her head; she wasn't a child who couldn't be allowed out on her own. 'I said it won't be necessary, Jordan—'

'And I've just told you it's no trouble,' he rejoined evenly, challenge in the deep gold of his eyes.

Stazy glared right back at him!

They might have continued their stubborn clash if Ben hadn't laughed softly. 'Met your match, Jordan?' he queried.

The irritation that flared briefly in those gold eyes, before Jordan quickly brought his emotions under control, clearly showed—to Stazy, at least—his dislike of Ben's teasing. And the reason for it.

But she was not about to be taken about from place

to place like a child in need of protection; she had had quite enough of that from her brothers over the years!

Jordan visibly forced himself to relax before turning to the older man, a wry smile on his lips. 'Stazy has a theory that all men are frogs—until proven otherwise.'

'And, so far, none of them have managed to turn into princes!' she returned firmly.

Marilyn gave a husky chuckle, obviously enjoying the exchange. 'My dear, you've been meeting the wrong men!'

Stazy already knew that, and if the men she'd dated hadn't managed to convince her, then her brothers had told her so often enough! 'You've just been lucky, Marilyn,' she returned noncommittally.

'Maybe, by meeting Jordan, your luck has changed...' the older woman told her optimistically.

She didn't think so. Oh, she enjoyed his company, and his kisses made her toes curl, but that wasn't enough to change her opinion concerning frogs. Especially in the company of Ben Travis!

'Stazy obviously doesn't think so,' Jordan said dryly as he was easily able to read her expression. 'And I can't exactly say I blame her, either,' he admitted.

She was sure he couldn't—not when both of them obviously remembered that the only reason he was out with her at all this evening was that she had unwittingly helped him out of a difficult situation with another woman!

'I can't imagine where you managed to find such a lovely young lady,' Ben Travis put in.

'He was just lucky,' Stazy returned, with a hard look in Jordan's direction.

He raised one dark brow. 'Having you live next door to me has nothing to do with luck,' he drawled.

'More to do with what apartments were for rent when I moved over here,' Stazy acknowledged, wishing the two of them could leave now.

They had all finished their coffee, refused refills—and she wasn't quite sure how much longer she could keep up this cheerful façade! She had received a severe shock a very short time ago, felt almost on the edge of hysteria—and if Ben Travis was any good at his job he should be able to realise that. If not the reason for it!

'Are you almost ready to leave, Jordan?' Stazy prompted. 'I have some curtains to finish tomorrow.'

Golden eyes openly mocked her. '"A woman's work…"' He deliberately provoked her.

Ordinarily, she would have risen to that provocation. But right now she just wanted to leave. 'They're your curtains,' she replied unconcernedly.

'Blackmail,' he accepted, signalling for the bill. 'I hope you'll excuse us?' He grinned at Marilyn and Ben. 'Stazy has some curtains to finish!'

Marilyn giggled. 'Beware the red hair, Jordan,' she warned.

He glanced at Stazy's fiery locks as he stood up. 'Perhaps it's dyed?' he said hopefully, eyes glinting with devilment.

'And perhaps your luck just ran out,' Ben murmured as he saw the fiery glitter in Stazy's eyes as she stood up. 'I thought dinner was on me?' he added lightly as Jordan dealt with the bill.

'I'm the one who got to spend the evening with the two most beautiful women in the room,' Jordan assured him.

Ben glanced at Stazy again. 'I think it's too late for you to salvage anything after your previous remark, Jordan,' he observed. 'And, as an uninvolved onlooker,

I have no doubts whatsoever that Stazy's hair is perfectly natural!'

'I know that,' Jordan said, picking up one of Stazy's hands and placing it firmly in his own. 'I just like to see her eyes flash when she's angry!'

He was going to see a lot more than her eyes flash if he continued to bait her in this way! But at least they were finally leaving, which was all she had really wanted.

'It was lovely to meet you both,' she told the other couple graciously, if not exactly sincerely; she had enjoyed Marilyn's company up until the point when Ben Travis had arrived. The last half an hour spent in his company had been pure torment!

'Our treat next time,' Ben promised.

There wouldn't be a 'next time' as far as Stazy was concerned. It wasn't even a possibility!

'I was only joking in there, you know,' Jordan said softly when they had completed half of their journey home in a taxi in complete silence. 'About the colour of your hair,' he added in explanation.

Stazy turned to him blankly in the semi-darkness, taking several seconds to realise what he was talking about; her thoughts had been miles away from here, and this man at her side.

That pause was long enough for Jordan's face to take on a look of impatience. 'Where have you gone?' he demanded to know harshly.

To another place, another time, *another* man.

But she didn't intend telling Jordan any of that. 'It's been a long evening, and I'm tired.' She signalled her weariness. 'Exciting too. Meeting Marilyn Palmer,' she commented as he continued to scowl.

'Don't worry, Stazy,' Jordan barked. 'I didn't for a

moment think you meant it was exciting spending time with me!'

Time spent in his company could be nerve-rackingly unpredictable, and she couldn't claim she was ever not aware of his complete maleness, because she was aware of him one hundred per cent of the time. It was just that other events this evening had overshadowed that awareness...

'Stop looking like the injured party, Jordan,' she returned. 'We both know I was your second choice of dining companion this evening!' But for a few well-chosen words from her earlier this evening it would have been Elaine sitting at his side in the back of the taxi!

He opened his mouth to say something, and then obviously thought better of it, his smile, when it came slightly forced. 'I'm glad you liked Marilyn. She really is a wonderful lady.'

Stazy gave him a sideways glance. 'I imagine Gaye is a lot like her mother,' she said half-questioningly, still unsure of how he felt about his newest sister-in-law.

Jordan shrugged. 'I really don't know Gaye that well,' he admitted. 'But if Jonathan thinks she's wonderful that's okay with me.'

That didn't sound as if he was in love with Gaye himself; in fact, far from it. So it had to be just weddings he disliked. Well, he was far from alone in that outlook!

Although Stazy couldn't help her feelings of relief at knowing it wasn't disappointment over losing Gaye that had made Jordan so bad-tempered at the wedding...

Was she actually starting to care about this man?

That would be pure stupidity on her part. Not just stupid, but ridiculous too. One thing she had learnt about the Hunter men during this last week was that they were as arrogantly sure of themselves as the Prince men were.

Out of the frying-pan into the fire? Not this woman; she had learnt her lesson, and learnt it well. Jordan was just another frog—even if he did behave like a chameleon most of the time!

'You're looking very fierce.' Jordan looked at her questioningly.

Not surprisingly, considering her thoughts! She forced herself to relax. 'I'm thinking about curtains,' she dismissed.

'Perhaps you should think about taking up another profession if it makes you look like that!'

Not likely; things were just starting to get off the ground for her. Thinking of which... 'There really is no need for you to drive me over to see Abbie on Monday—'

'I thought we had settled all that,' Jordan told her shortly, his mouth thinning with displeasure at having the subject brought up once again.

'Not by me,' Stazy returned just as stubbornly. 'Just how professional do you think I'm going to look to your family if you deliver me to their door like a child who isn't capable of finding her own way?'

Jordan's mouth twisted. 'I wouldn't worry about that too much if I were you—I think it's the personal side of your life that Abbie is more interested in!'

Stazy was well aware of that. But she was also confident enough in her own work not to be too worried about it. Abbie would quickly learn that Stazy took her work very seriously indeed, also that the work she did was of a very high standard. Hopefully, that would quickly be enough to steer her off the subject of Jordan...

'Okay.' Stazy showed her lack of interest. 'Please yourself.'

'I usually do,' he returned arrogantly.

So did she—which was where their problem lay. After a lifetime of bossy men Stazy did not want to actually fall in love with another one! 'The lady doth protest too much'…? Maybe she did, but it was the truth. Jordan Hunter was not for her. Even if he wanted to be. Which he most certainly didn't!

So why was she having this conversation with herself? Probably because she recognised the fact that she was already falling in love with Jordan…!

Which was a good enough reason to feel relieved when the taxi finally arrived back at their apartment building, Stazy instantly climbing out onto the pavement, Jordan's departure from the taxi much more leisurely as he paused to pay the fare.

'I was going to do that,' Stazy stated as he joined her. 'You bought dinner.'

'You can take female independence too damned far,' Jordan snapped, obviously at the end of his patience with her. 'Did no one ever tell you that men prefer it when a woman knows when to be feminine?'

'Oh, we told her,' drawled a deeply masculine voice. 'But as usual she didn't listen!'

Stazy had turned sharply at the first sound of that all too familiar tone, feeling the colour drain from her cheeks as she looked at the man who stood in the shadows. Nik!

The very last person she wanted to see—now, or at any other time!

CHAPTER EIGHT

JORDAN turned as a figure stepped out of the shadows, finding himself face to face with a tall, dark-haired man who stared back at him with the coldest grey eyes Jordan had ever seen, that arctic gaze moving over him critically before the man returned his attention to Stazy.

Another one! Also American, by his accent. How many more men were going to appear in Stazy's life?

Jordan could feel Stazy's tension as she took a step closer to his side, and the look on her face, a mixture of disgust and dismay, said she was no more pleased to see this man than Jordan was. So who was he?

'Nik,' Stazy greeted in a chilling voice that Jordan had never heard from her before. 'I don't need to ask how you found out where I was,' she continued scornfully. 'You sent the scouts on ahead!'

'I doubt they would appreciate being referred to as that,' the man returned derisively.

'Nevertheless,' Stazy snapped, 'that's exactly what they are! If you want them, they're at The—'

'You know damn well why I'm here,' Nik rasped harshly. 'And it has nothing to do with Rik and Zak!'

Nik reminded him of someone, Jordan decided slowly as he looked at the other man assessingly. He certainly spoke like him. He even looked a little like him too; arrogant and cold—Jarrett before he fell in love with Abbie and mellowed a little! But this fellow hadn't mellowed, the litheness of his body looking as hard as steel—and his heart along with it. How on earth had

109

Stazy—soft, bubbly, caring Stazy—become involved with such an aloof man?

Jordan put his arm protectively about Stazy's waist, his eyes narrowing in response to the look of fury that came over Nik's face at this act of intimacy.

'I have no idea who you are,' Jordan told Nik sternly, his arm tightening about Stazy as he felt her quiver in reaction to Nik's angry glare, 'but I know Stazy well enough to realise she doesn't want to see you!'

Heavy lids dropped over those icy grey eyes as the man looked down his nose at Jordan. 'And just how well do you know—Stazy? Or whatever she's calling herself nowadays!' he demanded, shooting her a scathing look.

Exactly what did Nik mean by that remark? Stazy was her name—wasn't it?

'Mind your own damned business, Nik,' Stazy was the one to bite back.

'You *are* my business,' Nik ground out tautly.

'It took you long enough to find me,' she responded challengingly. 'Don't tell me you're slipping, Nik!'

'Not in the least,' Nik drawled. 'I've known where you were from the moment you stepped on the plane in Los Angeles. I decided to leave you alone for the last three months to give you time to calm down.'

Jordan felt a quiver go through Stazy once again—but it was with anger this time, not apprehension! And if this man Nik knew her at all, he had to realise she was on the point of exploding—at him! Though it seemed very much as if he did know her; in fact it sounded suspiciously as if he had been the reason she'd left America...

'Well, it must be obvious to you by now that Stazy did a little more than calm down,' Jordan put in mockingly, golden gaze direct as the other man turned to him once again. No doubt that arctic glare and all that arrogance, usually daunted lesser men, but having grown up with an older brother from whom this man could be cloned, Jordan wasn't in the least intimidated!

'Who the hell *is* he, Stazy?' Nik wanted to know.

'Again, it's none of your business,' she returned fiercely, shooting Jordan a grateful look for his presence.

He was quite happy to give her his moral support against this overbearing bully—but he had some questions of his own he wanted answers to. He wasn't about to accept that it's-none-of-your-business line as the answer!

'I suggest that if you want to talk to Stazy you make an appointment,' Jordan told the older man firmly. 'Stazy is getting a chill standing out here—'

'Well, if she wore a little more perhaps she would be warmer!' Those cold grey eyes swept disapprovingly over Stazy's red dress. 'Didn't you learn your lesson the last time?' Nik rasped.

Stazy stiffened defensively. 'Jordan is nothing like Steve,' she protested. 'So don't try your bullying tactics on him—because they won't work,' she announced with satisfaction.

She was right about that—but who the hell was Steve? Jordan just couldn't keep up with all these men in her life! He wasn't sure that he wanted to, either...

'Jordan...?' Nik repeated slowly. 'Would you be Jordan Hunter? The guy who lives in the apartment next to Stazy's?'

'I would,' Jordan confirmed guardedly.

Nik nodded abruptly. 'Any relation to Jarrett Hunter?'

'And what if I am?' Jordan rejoined harshly.

The other man relaxed slightly. 'I know Jarrett. Quite well, in fact. He and I are old friends.'

Now why wasn't Jordan surprised to learn that? 'Perhaps you and he went to the same charm school?' he returned dryly.

Nik gave a wry smile, and then he chuckled. 'Yep, you're related to Jarrett, all right.' He put out his hand in greeting. 'Nik Prince.' He introduced himself.

Another Prince! Stazy's life seemed to be full of them. Had she kissed this one too...?

'Jordan Hunter.' He shook Nik Prince's hand, still eyeing him warily; being a friend of Jarrett's didn't make him any more acceptable in Jordan's eyes—especially if he were one of the Princes Stazy had kissed! Actually, he had a feeling Nik was the Chief Prince. He certainly acted as if he owned Stazy... 'Jarrett's youngest brother,' he added in grudging explanation.

'Well, isn't this cozy?' Stazy pulled away from Jordan now, moving away from both men, eyes flashing deeply blue.

That flashing blue that Jordan had remarked on so teasingly earlier this evening... God, was it really only an hour or so ago? His head was buzzing now—with Zak and Rik, this man Nik Prince, and another called Steve!

'Perhaps the two of you should go and have a drink together somewhere?' Stazy continued heatedly. 'Then you can compare notes and see if you have any other mutual acquaintances—*I* am going up to my apartment!' She took her key out of her handbag. 'If I go to sleep I might find all of this was a nightmare when I wake up again!'

'Oh, no, you don't, young lady.' Nik took a firm hold of her arm as she would have marched past him. 'I didn't come all this way to see you to have you walk away from me again,' he added grimly. 'I appreciate you're mad at me—'

'Mad at you!' she repeated forcefully, even her hair seeming to take on a brighter fiery colour in her fury. 'I'm not mad at you, Nik—I'm sick of you.' She gave a weary sigh. 'I'm sick of you being there every time I turn around, of you vetting my friends, of you trying to interfere in my work by acquiring jobs for me. I want to be me, Nik,' she stated emotionally. 'Not another extension of you!'

Nik's expression was grim. 'Stazy Walker isn't you,' he replied.

'It is now,' she affirmed, gently but purposefully removing his hand from her arm. 'I don't want you in my life, Nik,' she told him softly. 'Why won't you accept and understand that?' Tears swam in her eyes as she looked up at him.

Jordan's breath caught and held in his throat. God, if she ever told him to get out of her life in that way…!

But apart from a nerve pulsing in his jaw the man Nik looked unmoved by her pleading tone. Was he made of steel? Or could he just not take no for an answer?

'I'm not going to go away, Stazy,' Nik told her just as softly.

'Please yourself,' she said with resignation in her tone. 'You usually do anyway. Just stay away from me while you're doing it!'

The two men stood silent as they watched her walk over to the building, her head held high, pride in every inch of her tautly held body.

There were so many questions Jordan wanted to ask this arrogant man standing at his side. Who was Steve? What did Nik mean to Stazy? And if she wasn't Stazy Walker, who the hell was she?

But Jordan knew he wouldn't ask Nik any of those things. Besides being disloyal to Stazy, it would also invade her privacy; if she had wanted him to know about her, she would have told him.

But, his curiosity being what it was, it wasn't going to be easy not to ask Nik Prince what Stazy wouldn't tell him...

'How about that drink Stazy suggested?' Nik invited gruffly, obviously not as unmoved by Stazy's words as he had given the impression of being...

'No, thanks,' Jordan refused abruptly, turning to the other man, looking at him sceptically. 'She meant that, about leaving her alone.'

'I know it,' Nik confirmed grimly.

'And?' Jordan challenged frowningly.

'Can't be done, I'm afraid.' The other man shook his head. 'I made a promise to her mother that I would look out for her. And I keep my promises.'

To Stazy's mother... Was it possible this man was the father she so despised? No, Jordan immediately answered himself. Nik Prince, in his late thirties, wasn't old enough to be Stazy's father. Then who was he, if he had made that promise to Stazy's mother?

Except she wasn't Stazy...

What was her real name? And why had she changed it? It hadn't succeeded in helping her evade Nik Prince, if that had been the reason!

Jordan stood his ground. 'She seems to be doing okay on her own,' he told Nik pointedly; even those two difficult 'employers' when she'd first arrived in England, she had dealt with quite effectively.

Nik Prince's mouth tightened. '"Seems to be",' he repeated harshly. 'Ja—Stazy has a way of getting herself into awkward situations.' He paused. 'I'm not about to sit back and let anyone take advantage of her.'

Jordan stiffened. He had been mulling over what the rest of 'Ja' could have been—Janice, Janet, Jade, Jasmine?—but now he was more interested in what else Nik Prince had said...

'I hope that isn't a reference to me,' he said icily.

Nik looked at him speculatively. 'How much like Jarrett are you?' he asked.

'Very,' Jordan answered with certainty.

'In that case, it wasn't a reference to you!' Nik grinned across at Jordan.

When he wasn't being a nuisance to Stazy, Jordan knew Nik was probably someone he could like. But he was bothering Stazy, so the situation didn't arise.

'I'll tell Jarrett I saw you,' Jordan bit out tautly. He would also ask Jarrett what he knew about Nik Prince—that wasn't being disloyal to Stazy, was it...? Besides, he would like to know as much as he could about the enemy.

Nik Prince eyed him curiously. 'You don't have a clue who I am, do you?' He sounded amused.

'Not a clue,' Jordan confirmed offhandedly—knowing by the way the other man spoke that he should know him. That oversight would be rectified as soon as he could speak to Jarrett!

'Give Jarrett my regards when you speak to him.' Nik's derisive tone told Jordan he knew exactly what Jordan was going to do when he reached his own apartment. 'And the beautiful Abbie, too, of course,' he added with the first genuine warmth Jordan had heard in his voice.

Jordan hoped he didn't show that appreciation for Abbie in front of Jarrett; when it came to his wife, Jarrett was a very possessive man indeed. Although it might be interesting to see the clash between two such similar men…!

'I'll do that,' Jordan agreed shortly. 'Now, if you'll excuse me…' He turned and walked away.

'If you need to contact me, I'll be at the Waldorf,' Nik called after him.

Jordan turned back only briefly. 'I can't conceive of any situation in which that would be necessary,' he returned dismissively, using his key to open the outer security door, closing it firmly behind him; Stazy would not thank him if he unwittingly allowed Nik Prince access to her apartment!

What an evening! First Elaine—that seemed like hours ago!—then the dinner with Stazy and Marilyn, Ben belatedly joining them. And finally this confrontation with Nik Prince. As evenings went, this one had been far from—

All thought of telephoning Jarrett as soon as he got in went completely out of his head as he entered his apartment and found Stazy there asleep, her hair splayed out over the arm of the sofa, her hand folded against her cheek, her face taking on the innocence of a baby.

He might only have been ten minutes or so longer than Stazy in coming up to his flat, but it had obviously been long enough for her to curl herself up on his sofa and fall asleep!

Jordan moved quietly across the room, going down on his haunches beside her, gazing into her tranquil face. She was beautiful! Utterly and completely beautiful, and he realised he liked everything about her. Even the way she made herself so at home in his apartment! For a man who had always valued his privacy, that was quite an admission.

He wasn't falling in love with her—was he?

That thought made him recoil back in shock, sitting down abruptly on the carpeted floor behind him. He couldn't fall in love with Stazy— Hell, that wasn't even her real name, if Nik Prince was to be believed. And he saw no reason to disbelieve the other man. Besides, Stazy herself had said that was who she was *now*. But who had she been before? Would it make any difference if he knew?

Somehow he doubted it. He was falling in love with this child-woman—and he didn't like it one little bit!

CHAPTER NINE

STAZY was having the strangest dream. She was being chased by a tiger, a fiercely angry tiger that she couldn't seem to get away from, no matter how hard she tried. And the panic inside her told her that she wanted to get away very badly. And then another tiger appeared behind the first one. The second tiger had the most amazing golden-coloured eyes, eyes that held her mesmerised, freezing her where she stood. As she stood there, unable to move, the first tiger made a leap towards her, only to be halted in mid-air by the fierce charge of the second. She watched the two tigers fight, filled with horrified fascination, knowing that she would be damned whichever tiger won the ferocious battle...!

'No!' She sat up in panic, even as she cried out her protest, completely disorientated by her surroundings, recoiling in shock as her gaze encountered those fiercely golden eyes only feet away from her. The second tiger...!

'What is it, Stazy?' Jordan moved towards her.

She couldn't speak, could only stare at him. Jordan was the second tiger... And the first, relentless in his pursuit, had to be Nik...

'Stazy...?' Jordan watched her with concern. 'You were asleep. You must have been dreaming.'

She might have been, but that didn't make those dreams any less disturbing now that she was awake. 'Has Nik gone?' she asked huskily, swinging her legs to the floor as she sat up, pushing her tousled hair away from her face.

It had been a traumatic evening—meeting Ben Travis, Nik's unexpected arrival, the dream only seeming to add to her inner turmoil. Or maybe it was that inner turmoil that had created the dream? In some ways, at this moment, the dream seemed more real than reality...

Jordan's mouth twisted as he stood up. 'I presume so,' he replied tersely.

Stazy eyed him warily. 'What did he tell you?' She had come to Jordan's apartment with the intention of refuting anything Nik might have told Jordan after she'd left the two men alone together. But, instead, she had fallen asleep!

'Nothing,' Jordan assured her. 'I don't care to discuss you with a third party, Stazy,' he added flatly.

Nik hadn't told him anything? She shook her head disbelievingly—that didn't sound like the Nik she knew and loved. And she did love her eldest brother, probably even more than she loved Zak and Rik, but Nik's refusal to let her grow up had been slowly stifling her for years. She couldn't believe he hadn't talked to Jordan about her—if only to warn him to stay away from her. Nik had warned off every man that had come near her during the last three years, so why should Jordan be any different? Except Jordan wasn't like any other man she had ever met...

'However,' Jordan continued grimly, 'that doesn't mean I wouldn't like you to give me a few answers! Like—who are you? Because your name certainly isn't Stazy! Who is this Steve that I'm apparently nothing like? And what does Nik Prince mean to you?' he demanded.

If she answered all of those questions then Jordan

would know everything there was to know about her! Except the truth about her father... But that was something she didn't intend sharing with anyone, least of all Jordan...

She swallowed hard. 'Could I have a glass of water first, do you think?' That brief nap had totally befuddled her brain. But she must have been exhausted to have fallen asleep at all, especially so quickly.

'We'll both have a brandy,' Jordan decided firmly. 'You, because you need to wake up. Me—because I just need one,' he added self-derisively. 'You know, Stazy,' he muttered as he poured the two drinks, 'I was better off when you were just my anonymous next-door neighbour!'

She couldn't argue with that; of the two of them, Jordan had certainly fared worse so far in their friendship. She had acquired a job, with the possibility of a second one with his sister-in-law, whereas knowing her seemed to have created problems with the two other women in his life that she knew of—Stella at the wedding, and Elaine earlier tonight. It also seemed to have created difficulties for him with his family...

'You could always just try and forget you ever met me!'

He grimaced as he handed her one of the glasses of brandy. 'Impossible!' he said with feeling. 'As the saying goes, you're unforgettable, Stazy!' He took a swallow of his brandy, unmoved by the fiery liquid.

Stazy merely sipped at hers—brandy wasn't one of her favourite drinks at the best of times. And this wasn't the best! But Jordan hadn't looked in the mood for an argument.

'Answers, Stazy,' he demanded as he sat down in the armchair opposite her.

She drew in a deep breath. 'Jordan, I came to England to get away from all that—'

'I'm well aware of that,' he acknowledged heavily. 'But it seems to have followed you over here!'

'And I'm fully aware of that,' she sighed just as heavily.

'Look, Stazy—' he sat forward in the chair '—you must realise that Jarrett knowing Nik means I could go to my brother right now and get answers to some of these questions? But I would prefer not to; I would like to hear it from you. Are you married to Nik, is that it?'

'Married to him?' she repeated, incredulous. 'I'm not completely insane, Jordan—and any woman that becomes Nik's wife is going to have to be!' She was absolutely stunned that Jordan could ever have thought such a thing. The truth was preferable to that! 'Nik is my brother, Jordan,' she told him evenly. 'As are Zak and Rik,' she went on—heaven forbid he should imagine she was involved with either of them, either!

Jordan looked stunned. 'Your brothers? All of them?' He groaned disbelievingly.

He *had* imagined she was involved with Zak and Rik too! Who did he think she was, Mata Hari?

'All of them,' she acknowledged.

'Whew.' He whistled softly through his teeth. 'Nik. Zak. And Rik.' He blinked at the realisation.

Stazy gave an inclination of her head. 'Almost as bad as your mother with her penchant for Js!'

'Mmm.' He frowned, eyeing her speculatively. 'Your name wouldn't happen to be Jak, would it...?'

Her eyes widened. 'How did you—? Nik must have told you,' she said sharply.

'Not at all,' Jordan denied easily. 'I'll admit I did pick up on the "Ja" when he started to say your name earlier, but it wasn't too difficult to guess the rest. Jak.' He rolled the name experimentally around his tongue. 'I think I prefer Stazy,' he admitted honestly.

'So do I,' she said with feeling. 'If you could imagine the teasing I've put up with all my life because of our names—! My mother started her family in the sixties, and, once she had started off with Nik and Zak, Rik and Jak came quite easily to her!' Stazy shook her head. 'Why do parents never think further than the baby stage? I'm sure it was all very cute when we were young, but it isn't so funny now we're all adults!' She gave a despairing shake of her head. 'I prefer to use my middle name of Stazy.'

'But I don't understand why Nik is this protective of you,' Jordan said slowly. 'You're of age; you can do what you like.'

She gave a dismissive snort, the brandy having relaxed her somewhat. 'Try telling Nik that! He's been this way since our mother died three years ago.'

'Ah,' Jordan said understandingly.

Stazy gave him a quick look. What did he mean, 'ah'? Exactly what had he gleaned from her remark?

But she could read nothing from Jordan's expression. Damn him, he was as enigmatic as Nik himself!

She had come to Jordan's apartment with the intention of telling her side of anything Nik might have revealed to him. But, according to Jordan, Nik hadn't told him anything. Then why did she still feel at a disadvantage? She had been better off when she'd kept herself distant from everyone! One moment of weakness a week ago, when she had accepted Jordan's invitation out, and she was up to her neck in Hunters as well as Princes!

'Nik is the brother who taught you to appreciate a good wine,' Jordan guessed ruefully.

Nik had taught her a lot of things. Until a few months ago he had been her idol, the most marvellous man in the world, and although her senior by seventeen years he had always had time for her, playing with her when she was a baby, helping her with her schoolwork until she went away to boarding-school, visiting her often at that boarding-school, making sure she always felt loved and cherished, listening to her problems as she got older, helping her through her first unrequited love, drying her tears when she cried.

When had it all changed?

Why had it all changed?

She knew the answer to that all too well. It was something she could never completely forget, no matter how hard she tried. The day her life had changed for ever...

'Stazy, why are you crying?' Jordan whispered as he came down on his haunches beside her, reaching up to brush the tears from her cheeks. 'You don't have to talk about this any more if it makes you cry,' he soothed, taking her glass out of her shaking hand, putting both their glasses on the table before sitting next to her on the sofa, taking her hands into his much warmer ones. 'I don't want to hurt you, Stazy,' he assured her gruffly.

She looked up at him, her lashes still wet with tears. 'What do you want to do with me?' she said chokily.

He closed his eyes briefly as he drew her slowly towards him. 'I would rather show you than tell you!' he exclaimed before his mouth came down on hers, gently at first, and then more fiercely as his control seemed to crack.

It was as if Stazy had been waiting for this for days, her arms sliding up about his shoulders as she returned the kiss with a passion that matched his own.

It felt so right, so wonderfully right, their bodies fitting perfectly together as they moved to lie side by side on the sofa, Stazy's softness curving into the harder planes of Jordan's strength. And still he kissed her, his tongue moving erotically over her bottom lip, evoking sensations that left Stazy weak and clinging to him, and longing for more!

Jordan's hands moved restlessly up and down her spine, groaning softly as his hand moved to cup one of her breasts. Stazy welcomed his more intimate touch, the caress of his thumbtip over her taut nipple, warmth instantly engulfing her body, her lower limbs feeling on fire. As his hand moved, and his lips replaced those caressing fingers, it felt as if she might melt in those flames.

One of her hands became entangled in the dark thickness of the hair at his nape as she held him to her, the moist caress of his tongue against her turgid nipple sending spasms of delight through her whole body, her head buried back in the cushions as she arched up into that questing mouth and tongue, her breath coming in short, hollow gasps.

She had never known such consuming passion, such complete oneness with another person. It was as if she and Jordan were joined, and yet the restless movements of her thighs told her there was more. So much more...!

Any more pleasure than this and she was likely to lose her mind completely. If she hadn't already! There seemed to be nothing but Jordan and his warm caresses, and yet she knew—at least, she thought she knew— What did she know? Nothing. Everything. She couldn't think! She didn't want to think. What she wanted was to feel Jordan's body naked next to her own, to know his full possession, for their bodies to merge as totally as their emotions were at this moment. She—

'No!' Jordan drew back suddenly, releasing her abruptly, looking down at her with regretful eyes for the briefest fraction of a second, before he turned sharply away from her, swinging his legs to the floor before standing up and moving quickly away from her.

Stazy watched him uncomprehendingly. They had been so close—too close for Jordan, she realised dazedly; she looked at his rigidly closed expression as he stared sightlessly out of the window.

The pelmet she had half finished pinning up earlier looked slightly incongruous, she realised distractedly. Was it really only a few hours ago she had stood barefoot on that chair putting it up—? What did it matter? she chided herself as she directed another glance at Jordan's harshly set profile.

'I'm not that man, Stazy,' he suddenly rasped, not turning, his hands thrust into his trouser pockets, his shoulders set stiffly.

His words hit her with the force of a physical blow. She knew exactly what 'man' he was referring to. But she hadn't thought, hadn't expected—

'I don't want to *be* that man, Stazy,' he continued coldly. 'Save your innocence for the man who does!'

She had straightened her dress now, sitting up on the sofa, the heated colour in her cheeks of a few minutes ago fading quickly at the harsh cruelty of his words. He didn't want her! Not as she was, anyway...

'Say something, damn you!' He turned to her angrily, eyes glowing like molten gold.

What could she say? That it was him she wanted? That after tonight no other man would do? In the face of his anger there was only one thing she could say...

She stood up, relieved when her legs managed to hold her weight—she had feared she might crumple in a heap at his feet. 'Goodnight, Jordan,' she told him with quiet dignity.

'What?' he queried impatiently, scowling darkly.

'I said goodnight, Jordan,' she repeated levelly—amazed at her calmness when inside she was a mass of churning emotions. 'Thank you for dinner, and for introducing me to Marilyn Palmer; she was charming.' Stazy was regaining her confidence now, pride coming to her rescue. Her heart could break later. Once she was alone.

'Damn dinner. And meeting Marilyn,' he responded irritably. 'I just don't want to hurt you—'

'You've already said that,' Stazy reminded him dryly. She *was* hurting now, she could have added—but didn't. 'It seems I can't give my virginity away!' she added, self-consciously smoothing back the fiery tangle of her hair.

Jordan's face darkened angrily. 'It isn't something you should *want* to just give away,' he stated furiously. 'Somewhere out there—' he waved his hand distractedly in the direction of the world outside the apartment '—is a man who will appreciate your innocence, who will cherish it!'

'You're starting to sound like Nik now,' she scorned, at that moment wanting to hurt Jordan as he was hurting her.

Jordan flinched as the barb hit home. 'Then perhaps you should try listening to him occasionally!'

Her mouth quirked. 'I'll bear your advice in mind!' She turned to leave.

'Where are you going?' Jordan barked.

She turned slowly back to look at him. 'Home. To my own space. To my own bed,' she added pointedly.

A nerve pulsed erratically in his clenched cheek. 'What about the work you're doing here?' he grated.

Her brows rose. 'What about it? You surely don't want me to finish pinning the pelmet up just now?' she said, deliberately misunderstanding him. Because if he thought what had happened between them just now was going to prevent her from finishing the job she had started, then he was mistaken; she needed this work. And not just because the money she was paid for it would come in handy.

'Very funny, Stazy,' he returned wearily. 'You know damn well what I meant.'

She shrugged with much more nonchalance than she actually felt; inside she felt as if she was slowly dying! 'Unlike you, Jordan, I never confuse business with pleasure—and as you've told me there isn't going to be any more pleasure I'm quite prepared to get on with business!'

That nerve pulsing in his cheek had been joined by another one in his tightly clenched jaw. 'And what if I don't want you to get on with business?' he replied, obviously furious at her taunting tone.

Her eyes widened. 'Are you telling me that a Hunter's word isn't his bond?' She returned his challenge.

'You know, Stazy—' Jordan's tone was deceptively mild '—I think I'm starting to understand some of Nik's obvious frustration with you!'

'Well?' She ignored the reference to her oldest brother; she was not about to get into another conversation about him!

Jordan sighed, visibly relaxing. 'A Hunter's word is his bond,' he conceded.

Stazy shrugged. 'Then we don't have a problem, do we?' she concluded lightly before leaving. Because *they* didn't have a problem—*she* was the one who had that! And it was a problem she would have to learn to deal with. Alone.

Because she was in love with Jordan.

Totally.

Inexplicably.

Futilely…!

CHAPTER TEN

'YOU really have no idea who Nik Prince is?' Jarrett looked at Jordan incredulously.

'I wish people would stop saying that to me as if I were slightly simple or something!' Jordan bit out impatiently.

Jarrett grinned at him. 'Why stop at slightly? Okay, okay.' He held up a defensive hand as Jordan's scowl deepened. 'Why this sudden interest in Nik Prince?' he prompted curiously.

It was a curiosity Jordan had no intention of satisfying! Jarrett was already far too interested in Stazy and his own relationship with her; Jarrett certainly didn't need to know she was a Prince too, that Nik Prince was her older brother…

He looked casual. 'I met him briefly the other evening, and—'

'Nik's in London?' Jarrett cut in.

Jordan shot him a glare. 'I could hardly have met him otherwise, now could I?' he snapped. 'He told me to say hello to you and Abbie. So how do you know him?' And why didn't he, Jordan, have a clue who Nik Prince was?

He had racked his brains over the weekend as to who Nik could be, and he had still come up with nothing. The complete lack of noise or movement from the apartment next door had told him Stazy either wasn't at home or she wasn't in the mood for company. In either case, she was the last person he was going to ask for information about her brother!

He still couldn't believe how cool Stazy had been before leaving his place the other evening. He had still been struggling to get his riotous senses under control, and she had coolly suggested they get on with business! Business—when all he had wanted to do was carry her off to his bedroom and make love to her all night! Which was something, in the circumstances, that he could never do...

So he was left with only Jarrett as a possible source of information, and knowing Jarrett—as he did, only too well!—he wouldn't make it easy for him!

Jarrett continued, 'Do you remember the film crew we had in the hotel in Paris a couple of years ago?'

'Vaguely,' Jordan nodded; Jarrett had given permission for some filming to be done at one of the hotels they owned, as long as it didn't interfere with the guests.

'That was Nik. Nik Prince the film director,' Jarrett went on as Jordan still looked blank. 'Where the hell have you been the last few years, Jordan?' his brother scorned. 'Nik is a director of world renown. He won an Oscar last year.'

The film world wasn't one Jordan had ever been personally involved in. He occasionally bought and watched a video if it had good reviews, but sitting in a cinema, an overheated dark room, packed with people he didn't know, had never appealed to him...

'There are four Princes,' Jarrett continued, obviously warming to the subject now. 'Nik is the eldest and most well-known. Then comes Zak. He's an actor—'

'Has he won an Oscar, too?' Jordan put in sarcastically, recalling the blond, good-looking giant from

Stazy's apartment. But he hadn't known he was her brother then...

'Not yet. But he will,' Jarrett assured him with certainty. 'Then comes Rik—'

'Don't tell me,' Jordan drawled, 'he's an actor too.' Rik was the Heathcliff variety—tall, dark, and brooding, as Jordan recalled.

'Scriptwriter,' Jarrett grinned.

'And the fourth one?' Jordan tensed as he waited for Jarrett's comments on 'Jak'.

'Jak,' Jarrett confirmed. 'I've never met him, and I don't know too much about him, either. But I believe he's a lot younger than the other three. And I think he's involved in set designing.'

Him? Jarrett believed the fourth Prince was another male? And probably, with a name like Jak, it was a natural assumption to make... But Jarrett was wrong about one thing: He had met 'him'!

However, that wrong assumption also let Jordan off the hook; Jarrett had no reason whatsoever to associate the female Stazy with the male Jak. His own head was buzzing with all the information he had just received, so why confuse Jarrett too?

'Talented family,' Jordan dismissed vaguely.

'Very,' his brother nodded. 'But, with a father like Damien Prince, maybe that isn't so unusual!'

Jordan had been standing in Jarrett's office during their conversation, intending to keep it brief and casual, but he sat down now—before he fell down! Stazy's father had been *Damien Prince*? Even Jordan had heard of him! Although he had been dead for some years now, the man had been a legend in his own lifetime, a Hollywood actor with five-star quality, the winner of nu-

merous Oscars and other awards for his talent. *He* was
Stazy's father…?'

God, no wonder Stazy had been initially taken aback
at meeting Marilyn Palmer the other evening, but then
had seemed to take the whole thing in her stride. No
doubt stars like Marilyn had been regular visitors to the
Prince home during Stazy's childhood…

But Stazy had come to London on her own three
months ago, changing her name so that no one would
make the connection between herself and her famous
family. Now that family had tracked her down and followed her here. But why on earth had she run away in
the first place? Oh, he knew himself what it was like to
be the youngest in a successful family, the pressure that
could put on you, but he had never thought of leaving.
Stazy had told him she left because she wanted to be
herself, out of the shadow of her older brother. But
Jordan couldn't help thinking there was more to it than
that…

'No,' he agreed hollowly, filled with more questions
now than when he had started this conversation. The
other person he could ask those questions was unlikely
to answer them. In fact, after the other night, he wasn't
even sure she was still talking to him! This afternoon
would tell him that…

'So is Nik still in town?' Jarrett prompted again. 'Abbie and I met him only briefly in Paris—we were on our
honeymoon at the time, and I wasn't in a mood to share
Abbie with anyone, let alone that good-looking devil!'
he admitted ruefully. 'Abbie needs a bit of a treat—
looking after a small baby is hard work—and having
dinner with a famous film director could do it!'

'Abbie is not star-struck,' Jordan answered flatly, not
sure he wanted Jarrett to meet Nik Prince again…

Stazy's cover would be well and truly blown after that, and while he might not understand the reason for it he felt he should respect it. 'And if you think Abbie needs a pick-me-up why don't the two of you go away together for a couple of days?'

Jarrett's brows rose. 'Are you offering to babysit Conor?'

Six-year-old Charlie he could cope with, but a baby of a few months old was a different matter entirely...!

'Don't look so horrified, Jordan.' His brother chuckled at his obvious discomfort. 'Abbie would never be persuaded into leaving Conor when he's so young.'

'Very funny,' Jordan said dryly, standing up again. 'Anyway, I've passed on Nik's regards to you, now I have some work to get done before I leave for the day,' he pronounced.

Jarrett glanced at his wrist-watch. 'A little early, isn't it?' he responded.

Jordan shot him a glowering glare. 'Your wife has a meeting with an interior designer this afternoon; I've offered to drive Stazy there!' Although after the other evening he had no idea if his offer was still accepted!

'I see,' his brother said slowly. 'In that case, perhaps I should finish early too; I'd like to meet Stazy again,' he added goadingly.

Jordan didn't intend giving Jarrett satisfaction of responding to his taunt! 'Shouldn't one of us stay at the office and keep an eye on things?'

'In other words,' Jarrett correctly observed, 'you would rather I wasn't there!'

'Please yourself.' Jordan quoted Stazy's remark to her own older brother the other night. 'I'll be leaving in half an hour.' In time to catch Stazy before she could leave for her appointment without him!

At least by changing the subject so effectively he had avoided telling Jarrett where Nik Prince was staying while he was in London. Although Jordan didn't think Stazy, given her present coolness towards him, would thank him for it...

She didn't look pleased to see him at all when she opened the door to him an hour later, and found him scowling darkly as she kept him standing outside the door. At that moment Jordan felt about as wanted as her brothers must have done!

'I'm not late, am I?' he questioned as he strolled into her apartment—if he waited for her to invite him he would wait for ever!

He immediately noticed the material for his curtains spread out on her dining-table. That was a good sign; at least she was still working on them!

'Do we have time for a coffee before we leave?' he enquired as he turned back to face her, taking in everything about her appearance as he did so.

She looked as beautiful as ever in fitted black trousers and a black cashmere jumper, her hair loose down her spine. But she looked pale too; there were shadows beneath her eyes, as if she wasn't sleeping well. Of course that pallor could be due to the darkness of her clothing, but somehow Jordan didn't think so...

'I'll make you a coffee,' he offered firmly; she looked as if someone ought to take care of her!

'I can do it—'

'I'm sure you can,' he agreed softly. 'But I'm quite happy to do it for you.' He frowned even as he said the words; the trouble was he was quite happy to do anything for her that would take away the pain in the shadows of her eyes! 'Have you seen Nik again?' he guessed shrewdly as the two of them went into the kitchen.

Her mouth quirked ruefully. 'How did you guess?'

'Just lucky,' Jordan replied.

'He just left,' she admitted heavily.

'Permanently?

'Unfortunately, no,' she sighed. 'Nothing moves Nik when he has an idea in his head.'

Jordan glanced up from preparing the percolator. 'And this time his idea is…?'

Stazy sat down on one of the bar stools. 'For me to go back to the States with him.'

Jordan swore as he spilt some of the coffee on the work-top. And then swore again as he spilt some of the water on top of it. What a damned mess!

'Do you want to go with him?' Jordan kept his voice deliberately light as he wiped the work-top, but inside his thoughts were racing.

Stazy go back to America? Leave England? No longer live in the apartment next door? He would never see her again! Of course America wasn't quite the other end of the world, and with planes going back and forth every day she wasn't unreachable either. But if she was in America he could hardly do what he was doing now—just come in for coffee!

She pulled a face at his question. 'No.'

He was amazed at the relief he felt at her answer. 'Then you don't have to go, do you?' he said happily.

Stazy still looked far from happy. 'It isn't as simple as that,' she responded, looking very young, the freckles on her nose very noticeable against her other paleness.

Jordan left the coffee to percolate, perching on the bar stool opposite hers. 'I can't see what the problem is. If you don't want to go, then you don't go. Or is it financial?' His brows lowered as the thought occurred to him. 'Is Nik putting financial pressure on you?'

'No.' Stazy gave a wan smile at the idea. 'Financially I'm completely independent,' she explained.

'I suppose with a name like Prince you're bound to be,' Jordan realised; Damien Prince had been a star who could demand mega-bucks for the film roles he chose to play; of course his children would all be wealthy in their own right. So much for thinking that if she had a financial problem he could help her out!

'My name isn't Prince, it's Walker,' Stazy reminded him flatly. 'But my mother believed in women's independence, made sure I wasn't financially dependent on my brothers. No.' She sighed again. 'Nik's pressure is all emotional,' she continued. 'He claims that they're falling apart as a family without me there.'

Jordan was still caught up in her two previous statements; he knew she chose to call herself Walker, but that didn't change the fact that her name was really Prince. And why had her *mother* made sure she had money of her own? Why not her father? Unless her father had been one of those men who believed it was the males who should have the money?

But at her last statement Jordan abandoned those questions. 'They're grown men, for goodness' sake! All of them must be in their thirties? Surely they have their own lives to live without worrying about yours?' he cried as she nodded in confirmation of her brothers' ages.

The three Hunter brothers, although working together, had occupied their own bachelor homes—and the privacy to live their lives as they pleased!—as soon as they were mature enough, and rich enough, to do so. Surely Stazy's brothers were old enough—they were certainly rich enough!—to do the same thing?

'Oh, yes,' Stazy confirmed with a sad smile. 'But I

understand what Nik means. Until three years ago my mother was there to keep us all as a family, and after she died, as the only other female, I suppose I took over that role. I'm sure it must be the same in most families; without the parents there to keep it together, the children tend to go their own ways, and eventually they aren't a family any more.'

In a way Jordan could relate to that. He and his brothers had had little to do with their mother once she'd left, but their father was always there at the end of a telephone line, a steadying factor. But, even so, Stazy was a little young to be fulfilling that role!

'Surely they have their own friendships to pursue?' They had looked like three normal, healthily virile men to Jordan; surely they had relationships in their lives that didn't involve their young sister?

'Lots of them,' Stazy acknowledged wryly.

He moved to pour the coffee now it was ready. 'Then I really don't see Nik's problem.' Or maybe he just didn't want to,' The thought of Stazy leaving England didn't please him one little bit! 'Besides, you've just started to get your career moving over here,' he reminded her. 'Why on earth would you want to leave now?'

'I don't want to leave.' She took the mug of coffee he held out to her. 'I just—I have to think about this.'

'Well, while you're thinking about it, try to remember to take into account the reason you left in the first place,' Jordan rasped harshly. 'Don't just think about your brothers, your family, think about what you want too!'

Stazy gave him a quizzical glance. 'Careful, Jordan, or I might think you actually *want* me to stay here!' she taunted.

He did want her to stay here. And he didn't want to explain to himself—let alone Stazy—exactly why!

He half smiled. 'The tenant before you burnt joss-sticks and played weird music half the night—God knows who I would get next door if you left!'

For a few seconds Stazy just stared at him, and then she burst out laughing. And she carried on laughing. In fact, she couldn't seem to stop!

'Stazy?' Jordan said uncertainly. If she was hysterical then a sharp slap on her cheek should put an end to it, but if she wasn't and he administered the slap—! She had looked miserable enough before; she certainly didn't need him adding to her woes!

'I'm all right, Jordan,' she assured him as she slowly sobered. 'I've just never been described as preferable to joss-sticks and weird music before!' She gave a rueful shake of her head, still grinning. 'I should have guessed there was an ulterior motive to your telling me I should stay.' She stood up, moving to kiss him on the cheek. 'It's certainly brought me back onto the ground, re-minded me of just how unimportant I really am—'

'Now I didn't say that,' he put in protestingly.

'Not in so many words, no,' she replied, starting to look more like her normal self, the colour back in her cheeks, the sparkle back in her eyes. 'Nik almost got to me,' she admitted self-derisively. 'I should have remem-bered he was an actor before he decided he preferred directing.'

'He was?' Jordan was still recovering from that com-pletely spontaneous kiss on the cheek she had given him. Not that there had been any passion behind it, more like a kiss she would bestow on one of her brothers—not Nik, of course!—but he was still unsettled by the natu-ralness of it...

'He was,' Stazy grinned. 'He was pretty good too. But then, Nik is good at anything he chooses to do,' she conceded. 'I'm surprised you didn't recognise him and Zak. You aren't much of a movie-goer, are you, Jordan?' she teased.

'No,' he owned up reluctantly, sure that was another black mark against him in her eyes. Where Stazy was concerned he seemed to be notching them up by the dozen. And, for once in his life, it bothered him...

She gestured to the door. 'I won't be a minute; I just want to freshen up before we go to your sister-in-law's.'

And, like a breath of fresh air, she was gone. And Jordan could only stare after her, the room suddenly flat and uninspiring for lack of her presence.

There wasn't a single thing about Stazy that he disliked or found irritating, Jordan realised dazedly. He liked the way she looked, the soft lilt to her voice, her talent, her soft and caring heart—even when it came to her brother Nik, a man who had obviously caused her hurt in the past.

The problem was, Jordan very much doubted Stazy thought as favourably about him. He was bad-tempered, cynical, insulted her without even meaning to, and he knew little or nothing about the world her family inhabited. In fact, he couldn't think of a single thing for Stazy to like about him!

And he was very much afraid he wanted her to like him. In fact, he wanted her to more than like him.

Because he was falling in love with her.

Damn it, he was already in love with her!

Now what did he do...?

CHAPTER ELEVEN

SHE didn't just love this man, she liked him too, Stazy decided with a feeling of well-being as she sat beside Jordan on the drive back from Abbie's later that evening. He was warm and caring, and in the midst of his family he was the most relaxed and comfortable Stazy had ever seen him, holding Conor while they all looked at Charlie's bedroom, getting down on the floor to play with his niece when she arrived home from school and literally threw herself at him with a squeal of delight. For a man who denied wanting involvement himself, he obviously relished his brother's family life!

He was as confused about relationships as she was, Stazy had realised as she'd watched him that afternoon, a product of his own parents' failed marriage...

Not only did she love and like this man, she cared about him, and the feelings towards him that she had wrestled against acknowledging all weekend seemed to be growing, not fading. Nik had called her a fool three months ago, but surely falling in love with Jordan was the most foolish thing she had done to date...!

'Shall we stop somewhere on the way home and pick up a pizza or something to cook for dinner?' Jordan suggested lightly.

Her heart leapt at the thought of spending some more time with him, but caution held her back. 'Aren't you going out tonight?'

'If that's an invitation, I accept!' He quirked dark brows as he continued to drive.

'What happened to business?' She still held back, drawn towards spending more time with him, but fearful of making even more of a fool of herself.

'We can always talk about curtains as we eat, if that will make you feel better,' he returned dryly.

What would make her 'feel better' would be to have this man make love to her for hours, to fall asleep in his arms, and wake up there in the morning! But she would settle for dinner if that was all that was on offer at the moment.

'Okay,' she agreed. 'Where shall we eat?'

Jordan laughed softly. 'I like a woman who can make up her mind,' he explained at her questioning look. 'How about I surprise you as regards where we eat? We'll go home, change, I'll book a table, and—'

'You'll surprise me,' she finished. 'A word of warning. I don't like sushi, and I'm not into hamburgers!'

'An American who doesn't like hamburgers? Shame on you, Stazy,' he mocked. 'Okay, no sushi or hamburgers,' he accepted.

She was going to have dinner with Jordan! And she didn't really care where it was, or what they ate.

Stay away from him, she had warned herself over the weekend; Jordan couldn't have told her any more clearly that she would be wasting her time if she cared for him. But that caution became as nothing when she was with Jordan again.

'Fine,' she said as they reached their apartment building. 'But do I dress up or down?'

He gave her an uncomprehending look after parking the car in the underground car park. 'You look good whatever you wear,' he finally replied.

'Typical male reply,' she returned brightly, although she was inwardly pleased at the compliment. 'I doubt you would think that if I wore jeans and they frowned at my appearance in the restaurant you booked!'

'It wouldn't bother me in the least,' he said—and obviously meant it. 'But if you would feel more comfortable the dress you wore to the wedding will be fine.'

Dress up, she mentally decided. And she didn't have to wear the same dress; she did possess others. Quite a lot of them, in fact. At least Jordan knew who her family was now, so she could wear what she pleased and not worry about arousing his suspicions.

She knew by the way his eyes darkened with appreciation when she opened her door to him a short time later that she had chosen wisely in the black silk dress that fitted her like a second skin, her hair like flame against the dark material. Once again Jordan looked breathtaking in a black dinner-suit and crisp white shirt.

'May I say you scrub up very well, Stazy Walker?' Jordan told her with an appreciative grin.

'And may I say so do you, Jordan Hunter?' She grinned right back at him.

He lightly clasped her arm. 'Let's escape, before one of your brothers turns up!' he muttered conspiratorially.

'They do seem to have a habit of doing that, don't they?' she concurred, so happy this evening that she didn't think that even Nik's arrival could dampen her anticipation of the evening ahead.

Jordan himself seemed different tonight, that cloud of bad humour shaken off, that devilment he had warned her about very much in evidence. Well, that was okay with her; she was in the mood for a good time herself!

She was doubly glad she had asked him what she should wear when Jordan escorted her into one of the most fashionable restaurants in town! It was mentioned in the newspapers all the time as one of the places to go, booked up days in advance, and Stazy couldn't help wondering how he had managed to get a table for them at such short notice.

'My cousin has a table booked here every evening.' Jordan answered her query distractedly, seeming to be looking around the restaurant for someone.

'Your cousin?' Stazy prompted warily, wondering what sort of person chose to eat in the same restaurant every evening. And why...

'Mmm,' Jordan confirmed, still looked around the room. 'He— Ah, there he is,' he murmured with satisfaction, waving away the waiter who was heading in their direction, once again clasping Stazy's arm and guiding her over to a table near the window.

Stazy's trepidation grew as they approached the table and she saw the lone man seated there. She had thought she was spending the evening alone with Jordan, and now it looked as if she was about to be introduced to yet another member of his family. As the man seated at the table they were approaching turned and looked in their direction, Stazy felt the shock of recognition tremble through her body as she looked at his powerful build, the wings of grey at his temples in his otherwise dark hair. She knew this man!

'Gabe!' Jordan greeted him with obvious pleasure, the two shaking hands as the other man stood up.

'Jordan. Good to see you again.' The dark brown gaze was turned on Stazy as she stood rigidly at Jordan's side. 'And this is...?' There was a huskiness to his voice now, a definite flirtation in the darkness of his eyes.

'Behave yourself, Gabe,' Jordan warned as he too picked up on the change in his cousin. 'This is my friend Stazy Walker,' he introduced.

'Stazy...' Gabe said slowly as he took her hand in his, his gaze intent on her face.

'My cousin, Gabriel Hunter,' Jordan told Stazy. 'Just ignore him,' he advised as Stazy tried to remove her hand. 'He automatically goes into seduction mode as soon as he's introduced to a beautiful woman. You can let go of her hand now, Gabe.' There was a steely edge to his voice now as neither Stazy nor his cousin seemed to be taking any notice of him!

Because if Stazy had recognised Gabe Hunter on sight then she could see by the perplexed frown on the other man's face that he knew her too—he just hadn't been able to place where from. Yet...

It hadn't even occurred to her that Jordan could be related to Gabriel Hunter, the film and theatre critic! How could it have done? There had seemed no connection between the two of them. Except, of course, the name Hunter...

Gabe reluctantly let go of her hand. 'Shall we all sit down?' he suggested, but his gaze didn't waver from Stazy as they did so. 'I know you,' he suddenly said abruptly.

'Stazy was at the wedding with me last week,' Jordan supplied hopefully, the evening obviously not going as he had expected.

'No, it wasn't there...' Gabe said slowly. 'And somehow the name Stazy doesn't fit, either...'

What on earth was Jordan up to? came Stazy's furious thought. Why had he brought her here to have dinner with a man she didn't know? A man, moreover, who was respected internationally as one of the most acerbic critics of theatre and film that there had ever been! Her pleasure at spending the evening with Jordan died a quick and painful death.

'Don't be ridiculous, Gabe,' Jordan told his cousin sharply. 'I think Stazy should know her own name. Where's Wendy?' He changed the subject, not looking at Stazy as he did so—deliberately, it seemed to her.

Stazy's wariness was growing by the minute. At fifty-three, Gabe Hunter had a reputation as a hard and remorseless critic, had his own weekly television show in England, on which he proceeded, on most occasions, to ruin some poor actor's career. But he knew his business, never seemed to forget a film or play he had seen. Or—obviously—a face he knew!

'She left.' Gabe Hunter bitterly answered Jordan's question.

Jordan gave his cousin a knowing look. 'What did you say to her this time that she wouldn't even stay long enough to eat?' he said wearily, obviously knowing Gabe very well.

'I don't mean she left the restaurant,' Gabe answered hardly. 'She left *me*. At the weekend. She says she wants a divorce'

'Why?' Jordan prompted.

Gabe shrugged. 'Bad review.'

'You gave your own wife a bad review?' Jordan realised incredulously.

'Being my wife doesn't make her immune to reviews,' Gabe answered him with some surprise. 'She was bloody awful. I simply said so.'

While Jordan might find this hard to believe, Stazy certainly didn't; actors and directors alike lived in dread of this man criticising their work. But where a bad review could put them back into the realms of obscurity, by the same token, a good notice could boost their career to star level. But, even so, what sort of man gave his *own wife* a bad press? Obviously Gabe Hunter...

Jordan shook his head disgustedly. 'That will make three divorces in ten years, Gabe.'

'In eight years, actually, Jordan,' his cousin corrected him in a bored voice. 'But then, who's counting? Wives are like buses and taxis,' he continued scathingly. 'Never around when you want one, and then three arrive at the same time!'

From any other man this remark might have been funny, but from the acerbically dangerous Gabriel Hunter it wasn't remotely humorous!

'And, also like buses and taxis, if you miss one there will be another one along in a minute!' Stazy could hold back her own sharp retort no longer, instinctively disliking this man, and angry with Jordan for having put her in this intolerable position.

'Aha.' Gabe sat forward, a keen sharpness to his expression as he looked at her with narrowed eyes. 'You're American.'

'Very observant of you,' she snapped sarcastically, meeting his gaze unflinchingly.

Gabe's gaze narrowed even more at her vehemence. 'I don't think your friend likes me, Jordan,' he murmured mockingly.

'Probably because you're behaving like an idiot,' Jordan bit out impatiently. 'I had no idea you and Wendy had broken up when I suggested we have dinner together. This wasn't such a good idea—'

'Jak.' Gabe suddenly spoke out forcefully. 'Your name is Jak, not Stazy,' he murmured with satisfaction. 'You were at the Oscars last year with some young actor I— I remember now!' He smiled triumphantly. 'You were with Steve Somebody-or-other!'

'Barker,' Stazy provided through stiff lips, blue eyes glittering dangerously.

'That's right,' Gabe nodded. 'One of the lousiest actors I've seen in years!'

'So you said at the time,' she acknowledged tightly. 'Repeatedly. And loudly. To anyone who would listen.'

'Did I?'' He looked thoughtful, and then gave a dismissive shrug. 'It was the truth.'

It might or might not have been, but, whether it was or not, this man's criticism had lost Steve his next role in the film he had been hoping would launch his career on the road to starring roles. Nik had been the director of the next film Steve should have been in…

'Let's order some champagne,' Gabe announced recklessly, obviously not giving Steve—or his lost career—another thought. 'I feel like celebrating!'

'Not for me, thank you,' Stazy refused flatly, turning to Jordan. 'I hope you'll excuse me; I have a headache.' She stood up to leave.

'Named Gabe Hunter, no doubt,' Jordan realised as he too stood up. 'Go home and sober up, Gabe,' he advised harshly.

'I haven't even started yet,' the older man said grimly, signalling to the waiter and ordering the champagne.

Stazy paused beside the table. 'Has it ever occurred to you, Mr Hunter, that the higher you go, the further you have to fall?'

He looked up at her with hard eyes. 'It's occurred to me, Jak,' he drawled.

And been as quickly dismissed as an impossibility, Stazy realised, giving him one last contemptuous look before walking across the restaurant, her head held high, completely unaware of how beautiful she looked as she did so, her face flushed, her eyes blazing with anger.

What a jerk. What an idiot. What an absolute fool. How could anyone be so stupid? What on earth—?

'He's all those things, Stazy,' Jordan told her as they reached the pavement outside, the first she knew of him having followed her when she'd left the restaurant—or that she had been muttering those words out loud.

She turned to him furiously, shaking off the hand he had put on her arm. 'I was talking about *you*!' She glared at him.

'Me?' He stepped back as if she had physically struck him, looking absolutely stunned by the attack. 'What did I do?' he asked protestingly.

'You arranged to have dinner with that—with that *creep*! Took me there! Isn't that enough?' she declared.

'I thought I had arranged to have dinner with Gabe and his wife—'

'Who happens to have left him! And who can blame her?' Stazy accused knowingly.

'How the hell could I know Wendy wouldn't be there—?'

'Are you trying to tell me Gabriel Hunter is any less of a bastard when his wife is present?' Stazy said disbelievingly. 'I don't think so!' She was so angry she didn't even notice the curious looks of the people who passed them by on the pavement.

'I thought you would find him interesting!' Jordan defended sardonically.

'About as interesting as a mouse finds a cat—except this cat roars,' she bit out furiously. 'That man ruins people's careers, and consequently lives, just for the hell of it!' Her voice rose accusingly.

'I'll admit he can be pretty forthright when it comes to his job as critic—'

'Forthright!' she repeated incredulously. 'The man enjoys inflicting wounds and then watching people bleed! Doesn't what he's just done to his own wife prove that?

Any man with any decency at all wouldn't even have agreed to review his wife's work, let alone given her a bad one!' There were two angry red blotches of colour in her cheeks, the rest of her face pale. 'He—'

'I think we're deviating from the point here, Stazy,' Jordan cut in in a calming voice. 'The state of Gabe's marriage to Wendy really isn't the issue here—'

'It's a shining example of what a really first-class bastard he is,' she insisted vehemently.

Jordan tilted his head sideways as he looked at her consideringly. 'I think this is the first time I've ever heard you swear—'

'Gabe Hunter could make a saint swear!' She couldn't believe how angry she felt, all the frustration and pain of three months ago coming to the surface again.

'This man—' Jordan spoke carefully '—Steve, I think Gabe said his name was; what did he mean to you?' His eyes were on her face, questioning.

At the time, everything! Or, at least, she had thought he did. But then Gabriel Hunter had reviewed the film in which Steve had a relatively small part, had ripped his acting ability to pieces, and Nik, after reading those reviews, had decided not to use Steve in his next film after all. There had been a terrible row over it, and Steve had walked out of her life. For ever.

Oh, maybe it hadn't been as cut and dried as that, but the outcome had been the same. Steve had gone out of her life. And, once again, Nik had directed where *her* life should go. With help from Gabe Hunter...

'Everything!' she cried, still fired by the anger she felt at having come face to face with Gabriel Hunter. 'I was going to marry him!'

Jordan became very still. 'What happened?'

'Your cousin happened! And my brother happened!

What does it matter what happened?' she exclaimed. 'I obviously didn't marry Steve, after all!' The pain and humiliation that had gone along with that was what had made her leave America three months ago.

She had loved Steve, or had believed she did, thought they were going to have a wonderful life together. But within a matter of days it had all been over. Nik had been inflexible in his decision to drop Steve from the film he was directing, refused to listen to any of Stazy's pleadings on Steve's behalf. After that she hadn't even wanted to be in the same country as her oldest brother!

'Do me a favour, Jordan,' she continued emotionally. 'The next time you want to take someone out to dinner, give Stella or Elaine a ring—anyone but me! It seems that every time I go out with you I meet someone I would rather never set eyes on!' She turned on her heel and hurried away, flagging down the first taxi that passed and getting inside—sometimes there *was* a taxi there when you needed one, after all…!

CHAPTER TWELVE

NIK PRINCE didn't look in the least surprised to see Jordan standing outside when he opened the door of his hotel suite. 'I wondered how long it would take before you came looking for me,' he said, opening the door wider so that Jordan could go inside. 'Drink?' Nik held up a bottle of whisky.

'Thanks,' Jordan accepted, sitting down heavily in one of the armchairs.

He had run out of answers to his own questions ten seconds after Stazy left him, and, although he hadn't wanted to come and talk to Nik Prince, he simply didn't know where else to go. He needed those answers...

Stazy had been in love with someone called Steve Barker, had intended marrying him!

When she'd told him that it had felt to Jordan as if someone had dealt a blow to his chest, one from which he hadn't recovered yet...

He also had no idea what she had meant by that remark—'every time I go out with you I meet someone I would rather never set eyes on'. Who exactly did she mean? Oh, he could understand her not liking Stella and Elaine—he really would have to explain to her exactly who Stella was!—but he really didn't understand why she hadn't liked Marilyn and Ben. At the time, after her initial shyness, she had seemed to get on fine with both of them.

Admit it, Jordan, he told himself, for the first time in your life you're totally at a loss where a woman is concerned. Which is why you're here in Nik Prince's hotel suite…

Nik handed him his glass of whisky before relaxing back in the chair opposite him, cradling his own glass in his hands. 'What happened?' he prompted dryly.

Jordan shook his head dazedly. 'I wish I knew. Oh, I realised the problem with Gabe, once she had explained it to me, but—'

'Gabe?' the other man repeated with soft disbelief. 'You introduced her to your cousin, Gabriel Hunter?'

Jordan frowned at the other man's incredulity. 'You know Gabe too?'

'A little,' Nik confirmed in an amused voice. 'Which hospital is he in? I'll have some flowers sent to him!'

'Very funny!' Jordan grinned. 'He was still mobile when we left him,' he assured Nik. 'Although that could have changed,' he added thoughtfully as he thought of the champagne his cousin had been about to consume. 'He has women trouble,' he explained to Nik economically.

'There's a lot of it about,' Nik drawled. 'Oh, not me, Jordan,' he laughed. 'I have more sense than to get involved! Women have been nothing but trouble since Eve plucked that damned apple! But tell me, how long have *you* been in love with my little sister?'

'I have no idea,' Jordan answered honestly, knowing there was no point in prevaricating with this man; he was Jarrett all over again!

'Crept up on you, hmm?' Nik sympathised. 'I can understand that—she's all too lovable. I've loved her since the day she was born,' he admitted. 'A tiny little thing with bright red hair—and a yell that kept half the neighbourhood awake for months!'

Jordan grimaced at the image Nik portrayed. 'And you still love her?'

The other man nodded, the hard planes of his face softening with the emotion. 'When she wasn't yelling she had the smile of an angel. The sun seemed to come out when Jak smiled,' he recalled.

'It still does,' Jordan acknowledged morosely, wondering if she would ever smile at him again. After tonight, he somehow doubted it. 'Do you suppose she's still in love with this Steve character?' He frowned across at Nik, dreading, and yet at the same time needing to know, his answer.

This was definitely a first for him; he could never remember asking another man for advice about a woman before, let alone that woman's brother! But then, he had never been in love before, either...

'I personally don't think she was ever in love with him,' Nik answered hardly. 'Jak—had a hard time when our mother died three years ago, seemed to lose her own identity for a while, was searching for—something. She was pretty wild for a while. And then she met Steve Barker,' he confirmed. 'I knew what Steve was from the beginning, but if he made Jak happy that was okay with me. I just wanted my little sister back as she used to be. When she announced her intention of marrying the little—of marrying him,' Nik continued, 'I knew I had to set him straight about a few things. Marrying a Prince did not give him any special privileges where his career was concerned, and especially not with me!' Nik's eyes were as cold as ice, a pale translucent grey. 'Once he realised the truth of that he decided not to marry Jak after all!'

'Stazy—I'm sorry, but it's the name I know her by— she says you threw this Steve off your next picture after

Gabe gave him a bad review.' Jordan frowned his puzzlement at Stazy's anger with these two men; it sounded as if they had both done her a favour by showing this Steve in his true colours. Although it must have been humiliating for her at the time…!

Nik lifted his hands at the accusation. 'On the surface of things, that is what happened. Stazy is my sister, Jordan,' he defended, 'and I love her very much. There is no way I wanted her to know exactly why Barker was marrying her.'

'But surely, this way she believes you ruined that relationship for her?' Jordan responded. But at least he had the answer as to why Stazy had left America three months ago. And why she was so angry with Nik.

'When she calms down—which, admittedly, is taking rather longer than it usually does!—she will realise exactly what happened. Stazy isn't stupid—she's just damned stubborn!'

Her brother must love her very much to have accepted her anger towards him rather than humiliate her with the truth. Jordan wasn't so sure he could have been that generous given the same circumstances…

'So tell me,' Nik prompted with amusement, 'I'm prepared to play the waiting game—but what are you going to do now?'

Jordan had a pained expression. 'I was hoping you might be able to tell me that!'

The other man grinned at his obvious discomfort. 'I'm told that sending flowers sometimes works—although probably not with Stazy,' he conceded at Jordan's sceptical snort. 'Have you tried just telling her that you love her?'

Jordan recoiled at the suggestion. Tell her he loved her! He couldn't do that. He had never told any woman he loved her. Because until now he had never been in love…

'Her big brother might warn me off.' He attempted to make light of the subject, still backing away from admitting his feelings for Stazy. To anyone.

Nik looked at him unblinkingly for several long seconds. 'I don't think so…' he finally said.

Jordan's mouth twisted at the irony. 'Family approval is no good without Stazy's—and at the moment she's more likely to slam the door in my face than greet me with open arms.' Especially after the way he had behaved at the weekend! Stazy had been his for the taking, had shown that she wanted him in return—and he had thrown it back in her face. Although he certainly couldn't tell her big, older brother that!

'Have the two of you been to bed together?'

Jordan looked sharply at the other man, realising that Nik's relaxed pose was exactly that, that he actually missed almost nothing going on around him. And somehow he had been able to read some of Jordan's thoughts just now.

'No, we haven't,' Jordan replied evenly. 'But even if we had I don't think that's any of your business.' He met the interest in the other man's gaze unflinchingly.

Finally Nik gave the briefest of nods. 'You'll do, Jordan,' he drawled, leaning forward to refill both their glasses. 'Now all you have to do is find a way to convince Stazy of that!' he added with amusement.

All he had to do. It was the equivalent of climbing Everest. With just as much chance of success, as far as he was concerned!

He felt like a schoolboy, God damn it, standing outside the headmaster's study waiting for a reprimand, instead of outside Stazy's apartment waiting to see if she would answer his ring on her doorbell.

Get a grip, Jordan, he told himself impatiently. He was thirty-five years old, for goodness' sake; what was the worst she could do? Tell him to go away?

'Go away,' Stazy told him flatly when she finally opened the door and saw him standing there, still wearing that beautiful black silk dress that he had thought looked so sexy on her earlier.

But she didn't slam the door in his face... And she must have known it was him at the door before she opened it, because it was the internal bell he had rung.

She had been crying. He could see the traces of tears still on her cheeks, and her lashes were dark and spiky, still wet. Oh, God, he couldn't bear the thought of her crying!

'What do you want?' she choked. 'Something else for you and your cousin to laugh about?' she scorned emotionally. 'Well, go ahead and laugh, Jordan. This may be the last chance you'll have. I've decided to go back to the States with Nik.'

He drew in a harsh breath. 'Because of what happened earlier? I've never laughed at you, Stazy,' he told her forcefully, wanting to reach out and hold her, but afraid that then she really would turn away from him. 'Not with Gabe or anyone else,' he continued as she still didn't close the door in his face. 'I had no idea you already knew Gabe. The truth of the matter is, I—I thought that by meeting him you would realise I'm not quite as out of touch with your world as you might think.'

What a stupid idea *that* had turned out to be! Even if Stazy hadn't met Gabe before, and had reason to dislike him, he should still have remembered what a cynical swine his cousin really was, and should have instinctively known Stazy would not like him. What had seemed like a good idea, that 'surprise' he had promised Stazy, had been the worst mistake he had ever made with her. Though he had made many, it seemed. It seemed a long time ago since he had stepped out of the lift and noticed her for the first time too!

'My world?' she echoed uncomprehendingly. 'I don't understand.'

'You come from an acting family, a family deeply involved in films and—'

'But that world isn't real, Jordan,' she protested, still looking at him with puzzlement. 'This is what's real—what I've created here for myself.' She opened her arms to encompass the apartment behind her.

'Then why the hell are you going back with Nik?'

She took in a deep breath. 'Because he needs me. Because at the moment I need to feel needed.' The tears were back in her eyes. 'It was a mistake to come to England. I don't belong here—'

'Who says you don't?' he demanded to know vehemently.

She gave a wan smile. 'I do.'

What did he say to that? What could he say that would change her mind? Should he tell her that he loved her, that he wanted her to stay? And then what? The thought of marriage still terrified the life out of him, and Stazy didn't deserve to be offered anything less. Besides which, despite Nik's amiability towards him earlier, he doubted he would settle for anything less, either!

So he opted for, what was for him, safe. 'What about the work you've started here?' he rasped. 'My apartment? The bedroom you've agreed to do for Abbie today?' What on earth was he babbling on about? Stazy wasn't contracted to do any of those things. Couldn't he have come up with something a little better than that as an incentive to get her to stay? Not without compromising himself, he couldn't...

'Don't worry, Jordan.' Stazy smiled at him. 'When I said I was going back, I didn't mean immediately. I don't intend just to disappear overnight. I'm sure that if I tell Nik I will be returning soon he'll be satisfied with that. I'm going to finish off my work here first, and then I'll go back to the States.'

But she sounded about as eager to go back as he was to let her go!

Do something, Jordan, he mentally berated himself. Say something to stop her going. But he couldn't do it, wasn't ready for that yet. So when would he be ready? he challenged himself again. When Stazy had already gone, most probably, he realised dully.

'That's something, at least,' he responded, frustrated with this situation, but most of all angry with himself.

Coward, he chided himself. So you had a lousy childhood, your mother was a bitch, she deserted the whole family when you were fourteen; does that mean you have to spend the rest of your life avoiding emotional commitment?

It had worked for him so far. But how would he feel when Stazy left? God, just the thought of that made his stomach heave. How much worse was he going to feel once she was gone?

'Stazy...'

'Oh, dear—I forgot to tell you they're coming to take your suite away tomorrow!' she burst out suddenly, her hand up to her mouth in contrition.

'My suite?' Jordan frowned, diverted from what he had been about to say.

''Fraid so,' Stazy confirmed. 'You see, I don't do upholstery myself. They've promised to have it back to you by the end of the week,' she added hastily, chewing awkwardly on her bottom lip as she waited for his reaction.

There was time, was his inward reaction. Stazy wasn't going anywhere yet, not if she was still working on his sitting room.

'And just what do I sit on in the meantime?' he drawled mockingly.

She quirked her brows mischievously. 'I can lend you a couple of bean-bags—'

'Thanks—but no, thanks! I've never been too sure about getting back onto my feet from one of those damned things!'

She laughed softly. 'You're starting to sound like Nik now.'

'Heaven forbid!' he returned. 'Although I suppose I'm a lot nearer his age than I am yours,' he realised with shock.

How old had this Steve been? Not as old as him, Jordan was sure. Hell, if he sat down and listed all the minuses against him where Stazy was concerned—!

'Nik was born old,' Stazy dismissed, totally missing the point behind Jordan's remark.

Or maybe it didn't matter to her that he was years older than she was? Or that he was a cynic? Or that he had lost count of the number of women he had known since he was in his teens? Or that his cousin was Gabe Hunter!

What was there about him for Stazy to be attracted to?

'Have you eaten yet?' He spoke of something completely different, having now completely depressed himself. 'I know I haven't. After our earlier fiasco.'

'Your cousin is a very sad man, I've decided since meeting him properly,' Stazy said with honesty.

Jordan couldn't say he had ever thought of Gabe in that way, but with two, almost three failed marriages behind him, and a way of alienating everyone around him, Jordan supposed he was... Strange, he had always thought Gabe lived an interesting and exciting life. But, in retrospect, Stazy was right; Gabe was just very sad...

'Maybe Wendy will forgive him and take him back,' he said hopefully; Wendy was definitely the best thing that had ever happened to Gabe—if only the other man could see it!

'And maybe she'll have more sense,' Stazy pronounced. 'I have a pizza in the freezer I could cook for dinner, if you would like to share it?' she offered lightly.

If...! 'Aren't we both just a little overdressed for pizza?' he said wryly, both of them still dressed in their evening wear.

'This is the only way to eat pizza,' she assured him, pulling him inside her apartment before gently closing the door. 'You light the candles, and I'll put the pizza in the oven.'

It was the most unorthodox—and enjoyable—meal Jordan had ever eaten in his life!

Stazy even made sitting on the floor on one of those damned bean-bags, surrounded by glowing candles, eating pizza, seem fun! Or maybe it was just that he enjoyed being with Stazy, no matter what they were doing...

What *was* he going to do about loving Stazy?

CHAPTER THIRTEEN

SHE had no idea what she was going to say to him when he arrived. And she had been able to tell by the surprise in his voice earlier when she'd spoken to him over the telephone that he had no idea why she wanted to see him either. But she had thought about this very carefully before making that call, had decided this was what she had to do, that it was time to put an end to all the lies and deceit. But, even so, she had arranged for them to meet at her apartment, needed the security of her own surroundings when they spoke.

He had already rung the security bell downstairs, would be arriving outside her door any minute now. And she could feel her nervousness growing as the seconds ticked by. What would she say? How was she going to say it?

Why was she going to say it at all...?

Because it would actually change nothing, benefit no one. But, nevertheless, it was something she felt she had to do. Then it would be over and done with.

She froze as her doorbell rang, running damp palms down her denim-clad thighs, knowing her face had been pale when she'd checked her appearance in the mirror a short time ago.

Go for it, Stazy, she instructed herself firmly. She had already gone through in her mind the worst scenario, and even that hadn't seemed as bad as the nervous tension she had been under since she'd attended Jonathan Hunter's wedding reception with Jordan.

161

The doorbell rang again at her delay, and she moved with jerky steps towards the door, taking a deep breath before opening it.

Benjamin Travis stood on the doorstep, as tall and handsome as ever, with that white hair and those twinkling blue eyes, although his expression was quizzical as he returned her gaze.

'Good evening, Stazy,' he greeted lightly. 'You asked to see me, and here I am.'

And he was obviously wondering exactly why!

'Ben,' Stazy nodded, opening the door wider. 'Please, come in.'

'Nice apartment.' He looked about him admiringly once they were in the sitting room. 'No wonder Jordan decided to let you decorate his apartment. Does your call mean that you've reconsidered my suggestion that you give Marilyn and I some advice on our new house?' He looked at her questioningly.

Her mouth twisted wryly. 'I don't usually ask clients—even prospective ones—to come to me!' She shook her head. 'Please, sit down.' She indicated one of the armchairs, remembering all too well Jordan's comments about the impracticality of the bean-bags.

Although he hadn't seemed to have too much trouble getting himself up from one last night when it had been time to leave…!

Jordan. She wished he were here. But would he understand? Would anyone understand why she had to do this? Would Ben?

'I'll have to tell Marilyn about this visit, you know,' Ben told her teasingly as he looked up at her from the comfort of the armchair. 'Paying house calls on beautiful young women comes under the heading ''Honesty'' between engaged couples!'

And he was obviously completely baffled himself as to the reason for his being here! As well he might be. The two of them had met briefly the other evening, and now out of the blue Stazy had telephoned him and asked him to come to her apartment on his way home from work! No wonder he was baffled!

Stazy nodded. 'You must tell Marilyn what you think best; I'll leave it to your discretion.'

Ben pulled a face. 'Sounds ominous!'

She didn't return his smile. 'Not really.'

He settled back more comfortably in the armchair. 'And will you be telling Jordan about this meeting?' he said casually.

She knew the reason for the question, understood his curiosity about her relationship with Jordan. But, in all honesty, she had no idea what her relationship was to Jordan. They seemed to go out to dinner, with one or both of them backing off immediately afterwards, and then last night they had sat on her apartment floor and eaten pizza together, and then Jordan had left without so much as saying if, let alone when, he would be seeing her again!

She shrugged. 'I can't see any reason to do so, no,' she dismissed.

'Pity,' Ben murmured. 'Jordan is a very capable young man. Any parent would be proud to have him for a son-in-law. Do your parents live in America, Stazy?' He changed the subject conversationally as he saw her stiffen at the suggestion she might marry Jordan.

'No,' she answered abruptly. 'Do you have any children, Ben?' The conversation was incredibly stilted, but what else could it be between two complete strangers?

'No,' he returned as abruptly. 'Are we about to swap

life stories, Stazy?' he added lightly. 'If so, I think you should sit down too; mine is rather longer than yours!'

Again she didn't return his smile, and she didn't sit down either, giving him a perplexed frown. 'But I thought— Someone said you have a son?' She looked at him guardedly.

'Did they?' he returned mildly. 'They—whoever they were—were right; I did have a son. He died,' he announced flatly.

Now Stazy did sit down, her legs feeling suddenly weak. Sam was dead? But when? How?

'Stazy, I have no idea what any of this is about—' Ben's voice had noticeably hardened now '— but I think we might both feel a lot happier if you got to the point.'

She couldn't think what the point was any more, was overwhelmed by a terrible sense of loss. Which, in the circumstances, was ridiculous. 'When did Sam die?' she asked breathlessly, her gaze pained.

Ben sat forward, watching her intently. 'Fifteen years ago,' he told her gruffly. 'He was knocked over by a car and killed.'

Stazy swallowed hard, fighting feelings of nausea. She felt nothing but anger towards Ben Travis, but Sam had been different— She couldn't believe he was dead!

'Stazy.' Ben still spoke gently. 'Fifteen years ago you could only have been six or seven? Six,' he repeated as she mumbled a reply. 'How could you possibly have known Sam? And please don't insult me by telling me you didn't know him; you're exhibiting all the signs of emotional loss. Stazy, do you have any brandy or whisky that I can give you?' he prompted as he stood up.

She shook her head. 'I'm okay.'

'Stazy,' Ben said slowly. 'How did you know my son's name was Sam?'

She looked up at him sharply. He had said so himself—hadn't he...? No. No, he hadn't, she realised. But— 'Wine,' she said flatly. 'I have some wine open in the kitchen. Red. Or it might be white.' She couldn't think straight. 'There are glasses there too. I'll go and—'

'You aren't going anywhere,' Ben insisted firmly. 'I'll only be a minute or so.'

Stazy didn't even attempt to argue with him, using the few minutes he was gone to try and gather her scattered wits together. She had been so angry with Ben for so long, but learning of Sam's death somehow changed all that. Ben had lost too. She couldn't even begin to imagine what it must be like to lose your child. Your only child...

'Drink it,' Ben instructed when he returned with the two glasses of red wine. 'I had a feeling I'm going to need some of this too!' He explained his own glass before taking a large swallow. 'You still haven't explained to me how you could possibly have known my son Sam,' he prompted after several minutes' silence.

She drew in a deep breath, knowing the moment of truth had come. And that she had to take full responsibility for instigating this confrontation. She could have just left things as they were, but she had chosen not to.

She swallowed hard, looking straight across into Ben's frowning face. 'I don't know him. Never met him. And now I never will,' she realised sadly. 'But Sam was my brother,' she announced flatly.

Ben didn't move, continued to look at her, blinking several times, but seeming unable to speak.

'Sam was my brother,' Stazy announced more strongly.

Ben released his breath in a sigh. 'You're Barbara's daughter?' he finally murmured raggedly.

Stazy looked at him blankly. 'Who is Barbara?'

'Sam's mother. She—she left us when he was three. I thought—' He shook his head dazedly. 'But if you aren't Barbara's daughter, then—'

'I have to be yours,' Stazy finished for him, still meeting his gaze steadily, blue eyes looking into blue. 'Tell me, Ben,' she continued softly, 'before your hair went white, what colour was it?'

His gaze strayed to the fiery length of her hair, and then back to her face, to the blue of her eyes, the freckles across the bridge of her nose, wide mouth, stubbornly pointed chin. 'Who are you, Stazy Walker?' he finally breathed huskily.

'Until I was eighteen, and my mother became ill and then died, I believed I was Jakeline Prince. But before my mother died—' she continued talking over Ben's pained gasp of recognition at the name Prince '—she told me the truth. A truth my much older brothers had always known,' she added with remembered pain. 'Damien Prince, their father, had died two years before I was born, so he couldn't possibly have been my father!'

It was a time she remembered with double pain—that of losing her mother, and of seeming to lose herself too. She wasn't Jakeline Prince at all, the only daughter of Jane and Damien Prince, but the daughter of an Englishman called Benjamin Travis, the man her mother had met, and briefly loved, during a trip to England to get over the death of her husband.

Ben was staring at her now as if he had never seen her before. 'Jane had a daughter, *my* daughter…?'

'No, *not* your daughter!' Stazy's eyes flashed angrily. 'You gave up the right to call me that when you turned your back on us!'

Her mother's illness had happened so quickly, so lethally, that nothing could be done to help her, and shortly before she died she'd had only brief periods of lucidity. But it was during these times that she'd tried to tell Stazy about her father, how he had helped her over the death of her husband, how the two of them had come to care for each other, what a wonderful man Ben was, a gifted psychiatrist, a devoted single parent to his son Sam.

Stazy had been stunned to learn of her real parentage, the single photograph of Benjamin Travis that her mother possessed showing a tall, handsome man with prematurely grey hair. Stazy had looked at that photograph and despised the man who had fathered her and left her mother to bear the consequences of that alone.

But she had recognised him the moment she'd caught a glimpse of him in the crowd at Jonathan Hunter's wedding, and when he'd turned up to dinner as Marilyn Palmer's fiancé...! Meeting him on a social level had been something she had never even dreamt would happen!

She had never intended looking for the man who had fathered her, had come to England three months ago because, after her broken relationship with Steve, she didn't feel she belonged in America any more. And as she had been educated in England—for reasons she had been able to guess once she knew that her real father was English!—she had felt this was her second home anyway.

But meeting Ben Travis—either accidentally or any other way—had not been part of her plans for the future!

But, having met him anyway, she felt bombarded with questions she needed answers to. And she didn't feel she could leave England now without answers to those questions...

'Stazy—' Ben gently cut in on her thoughts '—what did your mother tell you about us? About me?'

'She was very ill before she died,' she told him emotionally.

But her mother had still talked of this man with such admiration. A man who hadn't wanted her or their unborn child...

Stazy looked at Ben accusingly. 'She wanted me to know about you, about the joy she found in your relationship, how you had cared for each other. But if you cared for each other—' Stazy choked '—why didn't you stay together?' And why didn't you want *me*? she cried inwardly.

She had been loved and cosseted all her life by her mother and her older brothers, but to find that her real father had rejected her before she was even born had thrown her totally. She had become quite uncontrollable for a while after her mother had died and she'd learnt the truth, had felt as if her whole life up to that point had been a lie.

'Life isn't always that cut and dried, Stazy,' Ben sighed, looking at her as if he still couldn't quite believe what she was saying. 'It's certainly never that black and white! Stazy, your mother was a wonderful woman, was the first woman I allowed even partially in my life after my wife left me. I cared for Jane very much, and I know that she cared for me very much too, that our relationship helped her through a very difficult time in her life. But—and I know this is the part you aren't going to understand!—caring and admiration aren't enough for a long-term relationship. We had both suffered a loss, mine in quite a bitter way, your mother's loss devastatingly final. We were both too emotionally raw to actually be able to fall in love with each other. But there are other kinds of love, and—and I believe your mother and I had that.' He nodded with conviction.

He was wrong; loving Jordan as she did, she did understand the difference between loving and caring. 'But what about me?' she groaned emotionally. 'Didn't the fact that my mother was pregnant make any sort of difference to—?'

'Jane didn't tell me she was pregnant,' Ben cut in flatly.

'I don't believe you!' Stazy told him vehemently. 'You—' She broke off as the doorbell rang.

The internal doorbell. Which could only mean one person. Jordan...

He hadn't said anything about calling in to see her this evening, but, as she knew only too well, Jordan was a law unto himself. But if she answered the door, what would he make of Ben's presence here, a man who, to his knowledge, she had only met once before, and then only briefly?

'I think you have to answer that,' Ben told her quietly as the doorbell pealed again, Jordan's impatience with her lack of response tangible in the persistence of the second ring. 'At a guess it has to be Jordan,' he added dryly. 'If it makes it any easier for you, you can always tell him I called round about the decorating—'

'My mother brought me up not to tell lies,' Stazy snapped at him, her eyes flashing angrily.

'Admirable,' Ben acknowledged lightly. 'In that case, I'll leave it to your own discretion what you tell Jordan.' He neatly turned her earlier remark, concerning Marilyn and his presence here, back on her, making himself comfortable in the armchair, also making it obvious he was in no hurry to leave in the immediate future.

Stazy shot him an impatient glare before going out

into the hallway, still reeling from the remark he had
made before the doorbell had rung and interrupted them.
Of course her mother would have told him she was pregnant! She had to have told him. Why wouldn't she have
done…?

'Jordan.' She greeted him distractedly as she opened
the door to him.

'Hi,' he returned lightly. 'I picked up some Chinese
food on the way home.' He walked straight past her and
into the sitting room. 'I'm sure there's enough for three,'
he added challengingly as he looked speculatively across
the room at the older man.

Stazy had followed behind him, thrown by the way
he'd simply walked in. But as she looked at him, at his
angrily set features, the deep gold of his eyes, the tangible tension in his body, she realised that he had known
Ben was here before he'd rung her doorbell, before he'd
stridden into her apartment so arrogantly…!

'Not for me, thanks,' Ben refused smoothly. 'I'm having dinner with Marilyn later. But you two go ahead,'
he invited, his gaze calm and steady as he met the challenge in Jordan's.

'It's a little early to eat yet,' Stazy told Jordan dismissively. 'Why don't you put it in your oven to keep
warm, and I'll join you next door in half an hour or so?'
When Ben had gone…

As she watched the dark fury that swept over Jordan's
set features at her dismissal she had the distinct impression he was going to explode…!

He drew in a deeply controlling breath. 'Are you sure
half an hour will be long enough?' he bit out with icy
sarcasm.

Stazy remembered those amusing stories—she hadn't
found them amusing at the time!—that she had told

Jordan, about when she'd first arrived in London, and realised he was drawing his own conclusions concerning Ben's presence in her apartment. Completely erroneous conclusions!

'More than long enough.' Ben was the one to answer him hardly, also attuned to the accusation in Jordan's voice. And certainly not amused by it!

'Fine,' Jordan snapped forcefully, his eyes narrowed. 'As you already seem to have started on the red wine—' his contemptuous gaze ran over the two glasses on the table '—I'll go and open a bottle to accompany our meal. I'll see you in thirty minutes,' he told Stazy harshly. 'Ben,' he bit out dismissively before turning on his heel and leaving, the door slamming loudly behind him.

Stazy was shaking so badly by the time she heard him leave that she had to sit down. 'He—I— You know what conclusion Jordan has come to about your being here?' she groaned, shaking her head in total disbelief of how complicated this had all become.

All she had wanted to do was clarify the situation between Ben and herself before returning to America. She hadn't intended telling Jordan anything about it, had been going to finish her work here, and then leave. Had been... Because she knew she would now have to give Jordan some explanation for Ben's being here, couldn't let him go on thinking—well, thinking what he was at this moment!

Ben gave a regretful shrug. 'Who can blame him? He's emotionally involved.'

She shook her head. 'Not with me,' she assured him firmly.

'Well, it certainly isn't with me,' Ben drawled mockingly. 'And I stand by what I said earlier, Stazy—even more so now! Any parent would be proud to have Jordan as a son-in-law.' He met her gaze intently. 'Even one coming into your life as late as this…'

As Stazy looked at him, at the honesty in his expression, those unwavering blue eyes, she knew there was something terribly wrong with the conclusions she had come to three years ago. Ben claimed he hadn't known of her existence, and as she saw that unflinching honesty in those deep blue eyes, the absolute sincerity in his face, she knew she had to believe he was telling her the truth…

'I think,' she said slowly, 'you and I have a lot of talking to do in the next thirty minutes!'

'Where the hell do we begin?' Ben groaned.

'My mother always said it was best to start at the beginning,' Stazy told him huskily.

He nodded. 'And she was a very wise—much wiser than I realised all those years ago!—and wonderful woman.'

At least they agreed on something!

CHAPTER FOURTEEN

WHAT the hell was Ben doing in Stazy's apartment?

Jordan had been asking himself the same question, in several different ways, for the last fifty-five minutes! And none of the answers he had come up with were in the least satisfactory!

He had opened the bottle of red wine as soon as he'd got into his apartment, the first glassful disposed of very quickly, sitting down to sip more leisurely at the second. Until the allotted thirty minutes had come and gone. And then forty minutes. And then fifty. It was approaching an hour now since he had left Stazy's apartment, and with his third glass of wine, on an empty stomach, he was well on his way to being drunk!

He had seen Ben's car in the car park downstairs as soon as he'd arrived home, had thought the other man must be calling on him, although he couldn't think of any reason why he should be. But Ben hadn't been waiting in the lobby for him, and he could think of only one other person in the building who might have let him in. Even then he had thought Ben must have pressed Stazy's bell when he'd found Jordan wasn't home yet, and that he was waiting there for him. But Stazy's delay in answering his own ring, her reluctance to let him into her apartment, the two glasses of partly consumed wine, had told a very different story...!

Only Jordan wasn't sure what that story was!

After years of being on his own, Ben had taken one look at Marilyn a few months ago and decided he was going to marry her. He couldn't be willing to throw all that away because of an attraction for a woman forty years his junior. Could he...?

The ticking of the clock on the kitchen wall wasn't a sound Jordan had ever really noticed before, but in the expectant silence that surrounded him now it seemed very loud indeed. Tick. Tock. Tick. Tock. The seconds, minutes continued to pass. And still Stazy didn't come.

What on earth could a man in his sixties and a young woman barely in her twenties possibly find to talk about for such a long time? If they were talking...

Jordan shied abruptly away from thinking they could be doing anything else. Stazy had told him she was an innocent, and he refused to believe that could possibly have changed.

But she didn't even know Ben. And, in retrospect, she hadn't seemed to like him very much during the brief time he'd joined them after dinner the other evening. So what was Ben doing at her apartment now?

This was torture! It had been over an hour now. And Jordan knew he couldn't stand this inactivity a moment longer, standing up abruptly. He didn't care what they were doing next door; he was going back there, would demand to know exactly what—

The doorbell!

Stazy. At last.

God damn it, now he was reluctant to go and answer his door to her! What explanation would she give for Ben's visit? She seemed to favour honesty, no matter how painful it could sometimes be, so Jordan knew that whatever explanation she gave it would be the truthful one. His stomach churned at the thought.

The scathing remark he had been about to make as he opened the door died a death in his throat as he looked at Stazy. Her face was very pale, but her eyes looked red, as if she had been crying. If Ben had made her cry…!

'I'm sorry I was longer than I thought.' Her voice was husky, her gaze not quite meeting his. 'I— It was—' She began to cry, softly, the tears falling unchecked down her cheeks.

Jordan gathered her up into his arms, holding her tightly to him as he took her inside and closed the door firmly behind him. 'What is it? What did Ben do to you?' he ground out harshly. 'If he's harmed you I'll—' He broke off his angry threat as she shook her head where it lay against his chest. 'Just cry it out,' he soothed as he sat down on the floor with her still in his arms. 'We can talk later.'

Quite how much later it was when Stazy finally stopped crying, Jordan wasn't sure; there seemed to be an awful lot of tears that needed to be shed. But finally she stopped, using the tissue he handed her to wipe her cheeks, before noisily blowing her nose.

'Has Niagara stopped falling now?' he teased ruefully as she sat up, looking down at him sleepily as she nodded. 'Feel like talking?' he prompted gently, knowing that if she didn't he was going to have to accept that. But he wouldn't accept the same reticence from Ben when he saw him next. What the hell had happened between them for Stazy to be in this emotional state?

Stazy slipped out of his arms to sit next to him on the carpeted floor. 'Do you like bedtime stories, Jordan?' Her voice was even huskier than it had been before.

'It isn't bedtime,' he pointed out gently.

She met his gaze unblinkingly. 'It could be.'

His breath caught in his throat as her meaning became clear to him. No! Not this way. This wasn't how he

wanted Stazy. If he hadn't known it before, he had realised this last hour—especially these last ten minutes as
she'd cried in his arms—that he wanted Stazy in his life
always, not just to make love to as she was suggesting
now, but to look after, to cherish, to protect.

'Does this story have a happy ending?' he prompted
softly.

She gave a wan smile. 'Don't all bedtime stories?'

He shrugged. 'Personally I always thought the Big
Bad Wolf got a pretty raw deal in *Little Red Riding
Hood*— Ouch!' He grimaced as she punched him lightly
on the knee. But actually he was pleased to see some of
her fighting spirit returning. 'Okay, a story it is.' He
deliberately omitted to say 'bedtime'... That would happen on his terms, or not at all, and he wasn't sure Stazy
would accept his terms...

'Okay.' Her arm rested over his knees as she sat at
his feet, but she turned away, looking at something
across the room. 'Twenty-two years ago—'

'I always thought these sort of stories began "Once
upon a time"...?' he teased, uneasy with the way she
was no longer looking at him. Was this story so bad she
couldn't look at him? Twenty-two years ago she hadn't
even been born!

'That's for fairy stories, Jordan,' she sighed wearily.
'This story is all too real.'

He rested his hand gently on top of her head, lightly
caressing. 'It won't make any difference, Stazy,' he assured her huskily.

She turned to him sharply. 'Difference to what?' she
prompted warily.

'Anything.' He shrugged dismissively. He loved this
woman, no matter what deep, dark secret she was about
to tell him.

She drew in a deep breath, turning her head away once again. 'This is all so difficult. I've had trouble coming to terms with it, so goodness knows what you're going to make of it!'

'Try me,' he instructed gently.

She nodded. 'As you know, my mother was married to Damien Prince. And they had three sons—Nik, Zak and Rik—'

'And a daughter named Jak,' Jordan put in lightly.

Stazy shook her head. 'No, there was no daughter named Jak. Or one named Stazy either,' she added as he would have spoken again. 'Jordan, perhaps it will make things a little clearer to you if I tell you Damien Prince died twenty-*three* years ago.'

He hadn't been altogether sure how long it was since the famous actor died, but he knew it was over twenty years... But if it had been twenty-three years, then he couldn't possibly have been Stazy's father. Then who was?

The truth hit him like a lightning bolt. Ben...!

'Yes,' Stazy confirmed as she saw his stunned expression. 'After Damien died, my mother went through the usual trauma of losing a loved one—numbness, denial, anger, and then finally acceptance. But that acceptance left her with a restlessness she had never known before. She came to England on holiday. I knew that much from my mother,' she told Jordan. 'Ben has helped me to understand what followed.' She glanced up at Jordan, before quickly looking away again.

It didn't take too much intelligence to work out that during her holiday in England Stazy's mother had somehow met Ben, and that Stazy was the result of that relationship. It also didn't take too much understanding to realise that, although Ben and Stazy's mother might have had a relationship, it had actually been for all the wrong reasons. Jordan knew that Ben's marriage had been a disaster, and bringing up Sam on his own had been no easy task, often resulting in loneliness. It followed that Stazy's mother would have been lonely too after the death of her husband. Not the best recipe for a successful relationship...

'It seems,' Stazy continued softly, 'that my mother and Ben had met before, several years earlier when Damien was in London playing the part of a psychiatrist; Ben had helped him with the background of playing the part. So when my mother came over here on holiday after Damien's death it was only natural for her to look up some old friends. Ben was one of them.'

And Jordan could guess that the relationship had progressed quite naturally from there. But still for all the wrong reasons...

What must Ben be thinking and feeling now, to suddenly be confronted with a fully grown daughter? Because he knew the other man well enough to realise he would never have ducked out of his responsibility to his daughter if he had known of her existence.

Stazy's mother must have been a very brave woman, Jordan decided. She had to have known Ben would never let her go back to America expecting his child, that if he had known he would have insisted the two of them marry. It must have been no easy decision for her, but with three sons of her own waiting for her at home she had chosen to bring their child up alone. In retrospect, it was probably the right thing for her to have done; marriages based on the existence of an accidental pregnancy were a recipe for disaster. Although that certainly couldn't have helped Stazy when she'd learnt the truth...

'My mother had a belief.' Stazy spoke huskily into the silence. 'She believed that sometimes people enter your lives for a brief time, effect the changes that need to be made, and then they or you move on, never to meet again. Her relationship with Ben, she assured me, saved her sanity. Finding out she was expecting me gave her a reason for carrying on. She insisted Ben was a good man, a wonderful man, but I—' She broke off, sighing heavily. 'When I learnt the truth three years ago I was convinced that he must have known about me. And that he hadn't wanted me. Or my mother.'

And Jordan could see how, after years of believing you were one person and you were suddenly told you were someone else entirely, it would completely throw your world off-balance. In the same circumstances, he was sure he would have felt as confused and upset as Stazy obviously had.

'And now?' he prompted softly.

'Now I have to reassess what I feel,' she admitted ruefully. 'Ben isn't at all what I imagined. And at the moment he's understandably very shocked. It can't have been easy for him to suddenly be told he has a grown-up daughter!'

'I doubt he will be shocked for very long,' Jordan assured her gently. 'It almost finished him when he lost Sam, and to suddenly be presented with a daughter— and such a beautiful and talented daughter too…' Jordan gently touched her hair. 'He has to be the proudest man alive!'

Stazy grimaced. 'I—I'm afraid I wasn't very tactful when I told him who I was. I— My only excuse is that I was a little upset myself; for the last three years I have believed I have another brother called Sam. When Ben told me he was dead, I—I just—' She swallowed hard. 'That must have been so awful for him.'

Jordan nodded, remembering that time only too well himself. 'Sam was Jonathan's best friend at university,' he explained. 'We all knew him, Jonathan most of all, of course, but— Hell, I can't believe you're Sam's sister and Ben's daughter!' He shook his head dazedly. 'It was confusing enough before, Stazy,' he added mockingly. 'But now we have Jakeline Stazy Walker Prince Travis! That's a hell of a mouthful,' he dismissed impatiently.

Stazy smiled, a little wanly, but it was as close to the real thing as Jordan had seen for some time. 'I suggest Stazy Walker will do—'

'And I suggest,' he cut in forcefully, 'that we scrap all those and go for Stazy Hunter!'

She gave him a startled look. 'I— You—'

'I'm asking you to marry me, Stazy,' he said less confidently; God, he hadn't blown it, had he, by launching this at her so quickly after her confrontation with Ben? 'I don't care whose daughter you are, whose sister you are—I love you, and I want you to be my wife. Will you?' He held his breath as he waited for her answer.

As the seconds ticked by he wished she would give him an answer, one way or the other, before he expired from lack of breath!

And his breath almost did fail as Stazy turned away, a pained look on her face. She didn't love him. Didn't want to marry him. He had waited thirty-five years to fall in love, to want someone enough to marry them, be with them for the rest of his life—and she didn't feel the same way!

'Oh, no, Jordan!' she groaned in denial as she turned and saw the unguarded look of pain on his face. 'I love you too—'

'You do?' He pounced eagerly, pain suddenly turning to joy. Until he saw the frown that marred her brow. 'What is it, Stazy?' He grasped her arms and turned her towards him.

'Sam,' she told him abruptly. 'Ben said— He explained— He's worried in case— Sam had a heart defect as a child, quite a severe one,' she explained hurriedly as Jordan frowned darkly. 'Ben's worried now in case—'

'That couldn't happen to us, Stazy,' Jordan told her fiercely as he stood up and pulled her up beside him. 'Fate couldn't be that cruel. I've waited all my life for you.' And he knew it was true! Only this woman would do for him. For ever. 'We've met. We've fallen in love. *We are going to get married and spend the rest of our lives together!*' He couldn't accept anything less.

He refused to!

CHAPTER FIFTEEN

'IT'S like a scene from the OK Corral,' Stazy murmured with amusement as she looked across the room.

'The Hunters meet the Princes.' Jordan chuckled at her side, his arm possessively about her waist as he too looked over to where his brothers had just entered the room, their wives at their sides, and came face to face with Stazy's brothers.

'Except this is our wedding reception.' Stazy snuggled into his side. 'And our brothers actually all like each other!'

Which was a miracle in itself, as far as she was concerned, especially as she had been convinced she was going to have another fight on her hands with Nik when it came to her choice of husband. To her surprise, Nik had given her a hug when she'd broken the news to him, before congratulating her on finally getting some sense—she should have known she wouldn't get away completely scot-free! But they had finally made their peace, and she had to admit she had known for months exactly what sort of man Steve was; her pride just wouldn't let her admit it—besides, it had become a habit with her to be angry with Nik!

But not any more. She was married to the man she loved, and couldn't be angry with anyone at this moment.

Not even Gabe Hunter, who had been invited to the wedding—minus his wife Wendy, who still had more sense than to return to him—on condition he behave himself. With three Hunter brothers present, and an equal number of Princes, he didn't have much choice!

'I don't much like the look of that matchmaking glint in Abbie's eye.' Jordan grimaced ruefully as he looked across at his sister-in-law. 'You do realise, with all the Hunters safely married now, Abbie may just start on the Prince brothers?'

Stazy laughed huskily. 'I wish her luck! I've been trying for years to marry them off, if only to divert their interest from me; and as you can see I've failed miserably.' Although she couldn't help feeling slightly proud of the three handsome—if unmarried!—men across the room who were her brothers. Maybe she could help Abbie a little with the matchmaking...?

'You look absolutely beautiful, Stazy.' Marilyn hugged her as she arrived at the reception from the church where Stazy and Jordan had just been married.

Stazy returned the hug. It was all still rather complicated, but since Marilyn had married Ben a couple of weeks ago the older woman was now her stepmother, and Gaye, as well as now being her husband's sister-in-law, was also her stepsister!

'Of course she does,' Ben agreed proudly, receiving his own hug from Stazy. 'And make sure you look after her, young man,' he told Jordan as he shook the younger man's hand. 'Or you'll have me to answer to.'

Stazy smiled fondly at the man who was her father. Although rather belatedly, he was taking his role as her father very seriously indeed, and he couldn't have been more proud as he'd walked down the aisle at her side to give her to the man who was to become her husband, Nik at Jordan's side as his best man; that had been Jordan's more than acceptable answer to the fact that Stazy had wanted Ben to be the one to give her away, but didn't want to hurt Nik's feelings by doing so. It had worked out marvellously.

In fact, the whole thing had worked out marvellously, much more so than she could ever have imagined when she'd come to England five months ago. She had found her father, and although she still felt sad at losing the brother she had never known she felt that she did know him a little now, Ben more than happy to talk to her about Sam. And those tests that Ben had insisted she have had turned out to be unnecessary; her mother, Nik had assured her, had been very conscious of the fact, in view of Sam's problems, that there could be something wrong with her baby daughter, and tests had been carried out shortly after her birth.

And now she was married to Jordan, was Mrs Stazy Hunter, as he had wanted her to be...

All the people she loved were now in this room. Jordan, of course, her three brothers, Jarrett and Abbie with their children, Jonathan and Gaye, Ben and Marilyn, Jordan's father and his wife—he had explained to her exactly who and what Stella was, and she understood exactly why he didn't want her at their wedding! Safely reunited with her third husband—courtesy of Jarrett's intervention!—Stella had had little interest in attending her youngest son's wedding, anyway...

Stazy had never believed she could be this happy, didn't think life could get any better than it was at this moment. And yet she knew, with Jordan at her side as her husband, that it would...

HARLEQUIN ◆ PRESENTS®

*invites you to see
how the other half marry in:*

SOCIETY WEDDINGS

This sensational new five-book miniseries invites you to be our VIP guest at some of the most talked-about weddings of the decade—spectacular events where the cream of society gather to celebrate the marriages of dazzling brides and grooms in breathtaking, international locations.

Be there to toast each of the happy couples:

Aug. 1999—**The Wedding-Night Affair,** #2044,
Miranda Lee

Sept. 1999—**The Impatient Groom,** #2054,
Sara Wood

Oct. 1999—**The Mistress Bride,** #2056,
Michelle Reid

Nov. 1999—**The Society Groom,** #2066,
Mary Lyons

Dec. 1999—**A Convenient Bridegroom,** #2067,
Helen Bianchin

Available wherever Harlequin books are sold.

HARLEQUIN®
Makes any time special ™

Look us up on-line at: http://www.romance.net

HPSOCW

Looking For More Romance?

Visit Romance.net

Look us up on-line at: http://www.romance.net

Check in daily for these and other exciting features:

Hot off the press

View all current titles, and purchase them on-line.

What do the stars have in store for you?

Horoscope

Hot deals

Exclusive offers available only at Romance.net

Plus, don't miss our interactive quizzes, contests and bonus gifts.

PWEB

HARLEQUIN PRESENTS®

Jarrett, Jonathan and Jordan are

An exhilarating new miniseries by favorite author

CAROLE MORTIMER

The Hunter brothers are handsome, wealthy and
determinedly single—until each meets the woman
of his dreams. But dates and diamonds aren't
enough to win her heart.
Are those bachelor boys about to become husbands?

Find out in:
To Woo a Wife
Harlequin Presents® #2039, July 1999

To Be a Husband
#2043, August 1999

To Be a Bridegroom
#2051, September 1999

Some men are *meant* to marry!

Available wherever Harlequin books are sold.

HARLEQUIN®
Makes any time special ™

Look us up on-line at: http://www.romance.net   HPBBROS

HARLEQUIN ◆ PRESENTS®

EXPECTING

She's sexy, she's successful... and she's pregnant!

Relax and enjoy these new stories about spirited women and gorgeous men, whose passion results in pregnancies... sometimes unexpectedly! All the new parents-to-be will discover that the business of making babies brings with it the most special love of all....

September 1999—**Having Leo's Child** #2050
by Emma Darcy

October 1999—**Having His Babies** #2057
by Lindsay Armstrong

November 1999—**The Boss's Baby** #2064
by Miranda Lee

December 1999—**The Yuletide Child** #2070
by Charlotte Lamb

Available wherever Harlequin books are sold.

HARLEQUIN®
Makes any time special ™

Look us up on-line at: http://www.romance.net   HPEXP4

 **HARLEQUIN®**
Makes any time special ™

In celebration of Harlequin®'s golden anniversary

Enter to win a *dream!* You could win:

- A luxurious trip for two to *The Renaissance Cottonwoods Resort* in Scottsdale, Arizona, or
- A bouquet of flowers once a week for a year from **FTD**, or
- A $500 shopping spree, or
- A fabulous bath & body gift basket, including **K-tel**'s *Candlelight and Romance* 5-CD set.

Look for **WIN A DREAM** flash on specially marked Harlequin® titles by Penny Jordan, Dallas Schulze, Anne Stuart and Kristine Rolofson in October 1999*.

RENAISSANCE. COTTONWOODS RESORT
SCOTTSDALE, ARIZONA

*No purchase necessary—for contest details send a self-addressed envelope to Harlequin Makes Any Time Special Contest, P.O. Box 9069, Buffalo, NY, 14269-9069 (include contest name on self-addressed envelope). Contest ends December 31, 1999. Open to U.S. and Canadian residents who are 18 or over. Void where prohibited.

PHMATS-GR

"Don't miss this, it's a keeper!"
—**Muriel Jensen**

"Entertaining, exciting and
utterly enticing!"
—**Susan Mallery**

"Engaging, sexy…a fun-filled romp."
—**Vicki Lewis Thompson**

See what all your favorite authors
are talking about.

Coming October 1999 to a retail store near you.

HARLEQUIN®
Makes any time special ™

Silhouette®

Look us up on-line at: http://www.romance.net   PHQ4992

Coming Next Month

HARLEQUIN PRESENTS®

THE BEST HAS JUST GOTTEN BETTER!

#2055 THE BABY GAMBIT Anne Mather
Matteo di Falco was falling in love with Grace Horton. But it
was Grace's friend who was determined to marry him, by
any means necessary. Matteo was used to getting what he
wanted, and this time he wanted Grace—not her friend!

#2056 THE MISTRESS BRIDE Michelle Reid
(Society Weddings)
The high-profile affair between Sheikh Raschid Al Kadah and
Evie Delahaye was in the media spotlight because their
families were determined to keep them apart. Then Evie
discovered why she *must* marry Raschid....

#2057 HAVING HIS BABIES Lindsay Armstrong
(Expecting!)
Clare had independence, a thriving law firm and a wonderful
lover in Lachlan Hewitt. She knew she loved him, but she
didn't know how he really felt. Then she discovered she was
pregnant. What on earth would Lachlan say?

#2058 MARRIAGE UNDER SUSPICION Sara Craven
The anonymous note suggested that Kate's husband, Ryan,
had betrayed her. Kate was determined to keep her man.
But while their marriage was in jeopardy, there was no way
she'd tell Ryan she was expecting his baby!

#2059 AN ENGAGEMENT OF CONVENIENCE Catherine George
Leo Fortinari seemed to be fooled by Harriet's
impersonation of her friend, Rosa. He'd even agreed to a
pretend engagement with Harriet. But Leo knew that the
woman in his bed wasn't Rosa—for the impostor was a
virgin!

#2060 GIBSON'S GIRL Anne McAllister
Chloe's boss, Gibson Walker, was sinfully gorgeous, but
Chloe had to resist him—she was engaged to someone else!
But the more she ignored him, the more he wanted her.
And soon it became a question of who was seducing
whom....

HARLEQUIN · FIVE DECADES OF ROMANCE · CELEBRATES

In October 1999,
Harlequin Intrigue®
delivers a month of our
best authors, best miniseries
and best romantic suspense
as we celebrate Harlequin's
50th Anniversary!

Look for these terrific
Harlequin Intrigue® books
at your favorite retail stores:

STOLEN MOMENTS (#533)
by B.J. Daniels

MIDNIGHT CALLER (#534)
by Rebecca York

HIS ONLY SON (#535)
by Kelsey Roberts

UNDERCOVER DAD (#536)
by Charlotte Douglas

Look us up on-line at: http://www.romance.net   H50I_L